"I don't know what you're up to, Sarah, but even if I slept with you, even if I made love to you until sunup and it was the best I ever had, it wouldn't change anything."

"Make love? Is that what you thought I was asking you to do?"

"It sure sounded that way to me."

"Then you don't listen too well, cowboy." Sarah sat up straight, this time holding the sheet so that all Cody could see was her face. "I was having a bad case of nerves and thought you were feeling down yourself. A little closeness sometimes helps, but I had no intention of—of being intimate with you."

Cody stared at her, his mouth open, his ego slammed down a peg or two.

"But just for the record," she continued, so angry she couldn't bite back her words. "If I had made love with you, it *would* have been the best you ever had!"

Dear Harlequin Intrigue Reader,

The holidays are upon us again. This year, remember to give yourself a gift—the gift of great romantic suspense from Harlequin Intrigue!

In the exciting conclusion to TEXAS CONFIDENTIAL, *The Outsider's Redemption* (#593) by Joanna Wayne, Cody Gannon must make a life-and-death decision. Should he trust his fellow agents even though there may be a traitor among their ranks? Or should he trust Sarah Rand, a pregnant single mother-to-be, who may be as deadly as she is beautiful?

Another of THE SUTTON BABIES is on the way, in *Lullaby and Goodnight* (#594) by Susan Kearney. When Rafe Sutton learns Rhianna McCloud is about to have his baby, his honor demands that he protect her from a determined and mysterious stalker. But Rafe must also discover the stalker's connection to the Sutton family—before it's too late!

An unlikely partnership is forged in *To Die For* (#595) by Sharon Green. Tanda Grail is determined to find her brother's killer. Detective Mike Gerard doesn't want a woman distracting him while on a case. But when push comes to shove, is it Mike's desire to catch a killer that propels him, or his desire for Tanda?

First-time Harlequin Intrigue author Morgan Hayes makes her debut with *Tall, Dark and Wanted* (#596). Policewoman Molly Sparling refuses to believe Mitch Drake is dead. Her former flame and love of her life is missing from Witness Protection, but her superior tracking skills find him hiding out. While the cop in her wants to bring him in, the woman in her wants him to trust her. But Mitch just plain wants her back....

Wishing you the happiest of holidays from all of us at Harlequin Intrigue!

Sincerely,

Denise O'Sullivan
Associate Senior Editor
Harlequin Intrigue

THE OUTSIDER'S REDEMPTION

JOANNA WAYNE

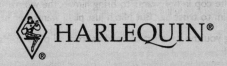

TORONTO • NEW YORK • LONDON
AMSTERDAM • PARIS • SYDNEY • HAMBURG
STOCKHOLM • ATHENS • TOKYO • MILAN • MADRID
PRAGUE • WARSAW • BUDAPEST • AUCKLAND

Special thanks and acknowledgment are given
to Joanna Wayne for her contribution
to the TEXAS CONFIDENTIAL series.

ISBN 0-373-22593-8

THE OUTSIDER'S REDEMPTION

Copyright © 2000 by Harlequin Books S.A.

ABOUT THE AUTHOR

Joanna Wayne lives with her husband just a few miles from steamy, exciting New Orleans, but her home is the perfect writer's hideaway. A lazy bayou, complete with graceful herons, colorful wood ducks and an occasional alligator, winds just below her back garden. When not creating tales of spine-tingling suspense and heartwarming romance, she enjoys reading, golfing or playing with her grandchildren, and, of course, researching and plotting out her next novel.

Joanna loves to hear from readers. You can request a newsletter by writing her at P.O. Box 2851, Harvey, LA 70059-2851.

Books by Joanna Wayne

HARLEQUIN INTRIGUE

*Randolph Family Ties

The Confidential Agent's Pledge

I hereby swear to uphold the law
to the best of my ability; to maintain the
level of integrity of this agency by my
compassion for victims, loyalty to my
brothers and courage under fire.

And above all, to hold all information and
identities in the strictest confidence....

★★★★

CAST OF CHARACTERS

Cody Gannon—Being a Texas Confidential agent meant everything to him until he learned why he'd been selected.

Sarah Rand—Has she sold out to the enemy or is she just an innocent woman running for her life?

Penny Archer—The Confidential agents' right-hand woman has a secret longing to get into the action.

Daniel Austin—A Texas Confidential agent for fifteen years, he was killed by Calderone. Or was he?

Tomaso Calderone—A ruthless criminal whom the Confidential agents have been trying to stop for years.

Elmore Cochran—The man whose office Sarah broke into to steal classified information.

Mitchell Forbes—The crusty, dynamic leader of Texas Confidential and Cody's hero—until he learned the truth about the man behind the badge.

Brady Morgan, Jake Cantrell and Rafe Alvarez— The other members on the Confidential team. Their allegiance is to Mitchell, and Cody is not certain he can trust them with details of his current mission.

Grover Rucker—Sarah's previous boss, recently retired.

Peter Rucker—Grover's son, but his sudden appearance at their hideaway has Cody and Sarah wondering if he doesn't know more than he claims.

Maddie Wells—A neighboring rancher and a widow who's been trying to get Mitchell Forbes to pop the question for years.

This book is dedicated to my friend Virginia,
who not only lives the life of a romance heroine
but is a true friend who makes me laugh,
even on my worst days. And to Wayne, always.

Prologue

Cody Gannon's boots clicked against the hospital's polished tile floors as he hurried toward Mitchell Forbes's room. The old warhorse was recovering and already raising cane with the doctors to let him go back to the Smoking Barrel. Not that anyone was surprised. A mere heart attack could never keep a man like Mitchell down.

Still, Cody had been scared to death when Mitchell had been rushed to the hospital with chest pains. The depth of his emotion had surprised him, especially since he was convinced he wasn't quite the man Mitchell had hoped for when he'd hired him on to work with Texas Confidential. The other three guys on the undercover team did no wrong. Cody seldom did anything right, at least in the critical eyes of Mitchell Forbes.

But the cantankerous old rancher-lawman had recruited Cody himself, offered him a position based strictly on his one brush with fame and heroism. He'd said he had faith in Cody's ability to handle the job in spite of his trouble-plagued past.

So Cody was living at the Smoking Barrel, had been for two years. The rest of the Texas Confidential agents weren't all that impressed that he'd foiled a bank robbery attempt and saved a young girl in the process.

They knew it was more instinct than bravery that had spurred him into action, but they'd welcomed him all the same and taught him what they could about working for the most exciting covert operation in the whole state of Texas.

No doubt about it, he owed Mitchell Forbes a lot for giving him the chance to be part of Texas Confidential and to finally make something of himself. He was going to make sure Mitchell knew that, and he was going to work twice as hard in the future to make the man proud of him. He picked up his pace, anxious to see for himself that Mitchell was doing as well as the others had reported.

He heard a female voice as he approached the room and recognized it at once. Maddie Wells, a neighboring rancher. He wasn't close enough to eavesdrop, but he could tell from her tone she was in her lecturing mode. Probably reading Mitchell the riot act about smoking his cigars. She was the only one who could jump him about his bad habits and get away with it. One day Mitchell was going to slow down a tad, and Maddie would snare him.

The door to Mitchell's room was open just a crack. He started to barge in but thought better of it. It was always a good idea to knock when a man was entertaining a woman, even if it was in a hospital room. He touched his knuckles to the door.

"Cody deserves to know the truth, Mitchell."

He hesitated, not sure he wanted to know any truth that brought that kind of seriousness to Maddie's tone. And if he was about to be canned, he sure didn't want to hear that.

"Give it up, Maddie."

Mitchell's voice was scratchy and Cody could picture

him in the bed, his muscles tight, his face drawn into stubborn lines. He waited silently, torn, knowing he shouldn't be listening in on a private conversation but knowing he couldn't turn away until he knew what Maddie was talking about. After all, this did concern him.

"Suppose you had died when you had that heart attack," Maddie said, her voice far softer than usual. "You would have gone to your grave without Cody's ever knowing the truth."

"That's the way I intend for it to be."

Cody's muscles tightened. He'd had his share of ugly secrets in his life, but he'd thought they ended when he'd buried Frank Gannon.

"Are you telling me that you have no intention of talking to Cody about this?"

"That's exactly what I'm saying. My biggest mistake was in ever telling you."

"No, your biggest mistake, Mitchell Forbes, was in walking away from your own flesh and blood in the first place. Cody Gannon is your son, and he deserves to know it."

Cody backed away from the door, but the words echoed in his mind, growing louder and louder until he wanted to scream at them to stop. He ducked into the stairwell and fell against the wall. He felt as if someone had slammed him in the gut with a two-by-four.

Maddie was wrong. He wasn't Mitchell Forbes's son. His father was Frank Gannon. He had the scars to prove it.

He took the steps two at a time, rounding one level and flying down the next. Scenes from his past reared up in his mind. Dark, ugly images that filled him with a dread so real he could taste it. Could taste the blood. Taste the fear.

But as quickly as they'd come, they were replaced by new images. Mitchell Forbes and his mother. He'd gotten her pregnant and walked away. Left her to marry Frank Gannon. Left her to die in her misery.

Cody reached the first floor and pushed out the door and into the stifling Texas heat. But it was not the sweltering heat that crawled over his skin and sucked away his breath. It was a bitterness so strong it destroyed his ability to reason.

All he knew was that if he never saw Mitchell Forbes again, it would still be eons too soon for him.

Chapter One

Cody Gannon picked up the glass and downed the bourbon. He seldom touched hard liquor, but tonight was special. A hard ball of emptiness had settled in the spot where his heart should have resided, and he needed the burn in his throat and the pain-numbing sting of the drink as it plunged into the pit of his stomach.

Cody Gannon. Illegitimate son. The words tore at his insides like crushed glass. Or shrapnel.

''Mitchell Forbes.'' He said the name out loud, rolled it over his tongue, spit it past the disgusting lump that had settled in his throat.

A week ago, the man had been his hero. But that was before Cody had found out the truth about Mitchell. That's why Cody's gear was in his pickup truck. All he owned. Amazingly little. Jeans, shirts, boots, a couple of jackets, his guns and a saddle. Even his horse belonged to Mitchell and Texas Confidential.

He had no idea where he was headed, wasn't even sure what town he'd stopped in. He didn't much care anymore, as long as it was far away from the Smoking Barrel.

Regret balled in his gut. He tried to force it away, but he hadn't drunk nearly enough to make it subside.

Being a part of Texas Confidential had been more than
a job. It had been his life. The first real commitment
he'd ever made to anything. The best friends he'd ever
had.

Now Cody had no choice but to walk away. Calderone and his band of murderous drug dealers would still
be stopped, but Cody wouldn't be in on the operation
that brought them down.

"Thank you, Mitchell Forbes." He downed the rest
of the bourbon and pushed the glass away as a bearded
man who smelled like he was two days past needing a
bath slid onto the bar stool next to him.

"Buy me a drink, mister?"

"I'd sooner buy you a bar of soap."

"Then save your money."

"Suit yourself." Cody stood and turned away from
the drunk, ready to move to another stool or one of the
tables in the back of the smoky saloon.

"You better save your money anyway. You'll probably need it now that you've walked off your job." The
stranger leaned over the bar, his hands spread out flat
on the marred wood.

Cody stopped and stared at him. His hair was gray,
thin and wiry, and his skin was bronzed and weathered
from hours spent in the sun. "What makes you think I
lost my job?" he asked, studying the man's facial expression as he waited for an answer.

"I don't think. I know." The man fingered the brim
of a soiled western hat. "Tell me, is Penny still as bossy
as ever?"

"I don't know any Penny," he lied.

"Sure you do. No one works at the Smoking Barrel
without knowing Penny Archer."

So that was it. The dirty drunk had probably worked

for a while on one of the ranches near the Smoking Barrel, though he didn't look familiar. It was no secret Cody worked for Mitchell Forbes. It was what he and the other Texas Confidential agents really did for Mitchell Forbes that was kept under wraps.

Still, the man made Cody nervous, and he might as well move on. He reached for his wallet and pulled out a few bills, enough to pay his tab and purchase one drink for the aging cowboy.

"You're not leaving, are you?" The man reached over and wrapped his fingers around Cody's left wrist. "I thought we'd get to be buddies."

"Think again."

"But we have so much to talk about. Mutual friends. A mutual enemy."

Cody smoothed the bills he'd tossed to the table, instantly aware of the change to the man's voice. He was no longer slurring his words, and his voice had lost all traces of frailty. He stared into the man's eyes, and experienced a vague sense of déjà vu. "What enemy would that be?"

"I was thinking of Tomaso Calderone, but I guess if you're not a *Confidential* anymore, you wouldn't be interested."

Cody swallowed hard. The man definitely had his attention now. No one outside of the powers in charge was supposed to know about Texas Confidential. The agents' ability to do their job depended on people believing that they were just everyday cowboys running a ranch. So did staying alive. He lowered his voice to a mere whisper. "Who are you?"

The man met his gaze. "Don't you recognize me, Cody?"

The voice was no longer disguised. It was smooth.

Easy. Almost familiar. He squinted, taking in the wrinkles in the man's face, his stringy beard, his wispy gray hair. The voice and the appearance didn't match. He only knew one man who could come up with a disguise that good, and this couldn't be him.

"I don't have any idea who you are or what you want from me."

"I'm Daniel Austin."

"Daniel Austin is dead."

"No. I'm too tough to die, though I wished for it a time or two." His lips curled into a half smile. "I was captured by Rialto's men, kept prisoner for months. Finally, I escaped, but by then, I knew enough about Calderone and how he worked that I was able to infiltrate his organization. I've worked my way all the way to the top. Calderone and me—we're like that." He indicated how close with two fingers on his right hand.

Cody shook his head. "No, Daniel is dead."

"Because that's what Mitchell Forbes told you? Believe me, that doesn't make it true."

Suspicion reared up inside Cody. He was supposed to be walking away from his life as a Texas Confidential agent, not being drawn into some secret conspiracy. But this man obviously knew all about them. And if he really was Daniel Austin... "Why would Mitchell be told you were dead if you're not?"

"You know the head honchos. They don't trust anyone."

"They trust Mitchell Forbes."

"Don't be so sure."

Cody tried to digest that last bit of information, but it boggled his mind. No one had ever infiltrated Calderone's circle. And if someone did, and Calderone found out, the man's body would be found in tiny pieces. Still, if anyone could do it, it would be Daniel Austin.

"So, if you're so close to Calderone, what in the hell are you doing here?"

"My job. But I can't do it alone."

"Then you need to talk to Rafe or one of the others. I'm out." Damn, here he was giving away information. The man was blowing his mind. He knew too much, but he couldn't be Daniel Austin. Or could he?

"Listen, Cody. I know what you're thinking, but you're wrong. I didn't just happen into this bar tonight. I followed you here. I need you. But before I give you the assignment, I have to be certain you're not going to go running back to Mitchell Forbes."

"Why's that?"

Daniel, or at least the man claiming to be Daniel, stared straight ahead, his back still hunched, his head still low, as if he really were an elderly man. He didn't face Cody when he talked, but when he paused, his Adam's apple rode up and down like it was bobbing in a pail of water.

"As you know, someone has been leaking secrets to Calderone. We think it might be Mitchell himself."

A curl of smoke from the cigarette of a man a few stools down wafted into Cody's face. His eyes burned, but not nearly as severely as the acid that pooled in his stomach. There was a leak somewhere. That part was true. But, Mitchell?

Even as angry as Cody was with the man, he'd never imagined Mitchell capable of deceit where Texas Confidential was concerned. Not when stopping Calderone seemed to be the cause that fueled his incredible drive.

But this would be just like the department. The same minds that had dreamed up Texas Confidential would like nothing better than having Daniel Austin, their master of disguises, working so far undercover that even Calderone himself would take the man into his confidence.

"What is it you need me to do?" he asked, still suspicious, but warming to the idea of getting in on the action of bringing Calderone down. Especially when it meant he'd outdo Mitchell Forbes.

"I need you to go to the airport and pick up a woman named Sarah Rand. She'll be flying into San Antonio and arriving at five o'clock tomorrow afternoon. After you pick her up, I'll contact you and tell you where I'll meet the two of you."

"And who is this Sarah Rand?"

"She's a secretary for the Department of Public Safety. Works for Elmore Cochran."

Cody recognized the name though he'd never met the man. He'd just been promoted and was now the final authority over anything involving Confidential agents.

Dan leaned in closer, his voice lowered to a barely audible whisper. "Evidence indicates that Miss Rand may have been selling secrets to Calderone, and that's what she thinks she's doing now. I've offered her one million dollars to deliver some secret files to me. If she delivers, it will prove her guilt."

Cody parted his lips as a low whistle escaped. "I don't see how this would prove anything except that she can be bribed for a million dollars. Selling you top secret info now doesn't mean she's done it before. Not to mention that there are laws against entrapment."

"You let me and the department worry about that end of it. All I need from you is a simple yes or no."

There was nothing simple about the answer Cody was about to give. If this man was Daniel Austin, then a yes would put Cody into the thick of things. He could be a major player in the action that brought the mighty Tomaso Calderone to his knees. And how sweet it would be to let Mitchell Forbes see that he was his own man.

But if this wasn't Daniel Austin, then he could be walking into a trap. He'd have to watch his back every minute. Nothing new there.

"I'll go with the yes."

Daniel nodded and his eyes warmed, though his lips stayed drawn in the same thin line.

"So after I pick up Miss Sarah Rand, where do I deliver her?" Cody asked.

"I'll let you know that at the time."

"How do I reach you?"

"You don't. I'll reach you. You just pick up the woman and get her into your truck. I'll make the connection at that point."

"I don't have a cellular phone anymore. The one I had belonged to Texas Confidential and I turned it in when I left. All I have is a beeper, and that only until someone cancels the contract."

"Then I guess that will have to do."

Cody scribbled his pager number down on a napkin and handed it to Daniel though he had the sneaking suspicion the man already knew it. "How will I recognize this woman?"

"She's young—in her twenties. Her hair's a reddish blond and she wears it straight and just long enough to cover her ears. She'll be wearing a hot pink suit." Daniel stood up. "Oh yeah," he added. "She'll be carrying a canvas tote that says 'So many cowboys, so little time.' You can't miss her."

With that, Daniel Austin slid off his stool and staggered to the door, doing a flawless performance as an elderly drunk. His baggy pants rode his thin hips, and the back of his gray hair zigzagged in and out of his shirt collar. One of the younger cowboys moved out of his way in deference to the man's apparent age and condition.

Cody waited a few minutes, then left the bar and walked back to his pickup truck. A few minutes ago, he'd been wallowing in his bad luck. But now the old juices were starting to flow. He was back in the saddle again.

CODY STOOD aside as the first eager passengers from Flight 109 made it to the end of the exit ramp. A few men and women in business suits, a hot-looking babe in a pair of skintight jeans, a group of elderly ladies all laughing as if they didn't have a care in the world.

The stream of arriving passengers slowed, and doubt started to nag at the back of his mind. If this turned out to be a fishing trip to a dry creek, he was going to be downright mad at himself. He craned his neck at the first sight of hot pink. Nope. False alarm. The woman was pregnant.

The hair color fit though. Hers was shiny, strawberry blond, straight. And just long enough to brush the edges of her blushed cheeks. Dressed in hot pink with a black coat and a leather purse draped over her shoulder and pulling a wheeled carry-on bag. Cute as a button, *but* pregnant, and Dan would surely have mentioned it if Cody was supposed to pick up a pregnant woman.

She stopped a few feet away from him and looked around. Cody expected some young, expectant father to rush up to meet her. No one did, and he couldn't help but notice the worry that creased her forehead and shaded her gorgeous green eyes.

She turned, and that's when Cody saw the cloth tote bag swinging from beneath the coat. The inscription was there, just like Dan had said. *So many cowboys, so little time.*

Undoubtedly this was Sarah Rand. Now all Cody had to do was pick her up and take her to meet Dan so that she could be arrested. Some hero he was, apprehending a pregnant lady.

Cody backed away and then stopped. Pregnant or not, if Sarah Rand was selling secrets that could give Calderone the winning edge, she had to be stopped. He only wished she looked like Calderone or like his right-arm man Rialto had. Those were the kind of criminals a man could get his kicks from sending to prison.

He walked over and tipped his Stetson. ''Mind if I help you, Mrs. Rand?''

She stared at him, then looked away, nervously scanning the crowd. Hot pink outfit, tote bag. It had to be her, so why was she ignoring him? He stood his ground. ''You are Mrs. Rand, aren't you?''

Her brows furrowed. ''Why do you ask?''

''I was sent to pick you up.''

She smiled slightly. ''You're not what I expected,'' she whispered, turning to glance over her shoulder.

''You don't have to whisper,'' Cody said. ''We're just a couple of friends meeting in the airport. Try to appear that way.''

''Okay.'' She took a deep breath, but didn't relax. ''I know I'm supposed to act cool, but ever since I caught the plane in D.C. I've been a nervous wreck. The man sitting next to me kept trying to talk to me and I finally told him I had a migraine just so he'd back off. I thought about telling him I was married to a very jealous husband but I don't wear a ring. I mean I'm pregnant and all but..."

"Okay, let's take it easy here. I'm a cowboy. We talk and *listen* nice and slow."

"I'm sorry. It's just that I've been so worried. I mean this is the first time I've ever done anything like this. I'm usually very calm, in perfect control. Well, maybe not calm, but better than this." Her eyes darted from one side of the terminal to the other. "I'm not afraid or anything. Well, actually, I am a little scared, but it's just because this is, well, you know, like stepping into a James Bond movie. Not that I think I'm a femme fatale. I didn't mean that."

He shook his head to clear it. If she talked this fast all the time, he'd grow dizzy trying to follow her. "Actually, it probably would be better if we saved the talk for later. Do you have the diskette?"

Her manner changed, grew suspicious. She tilted her head to one side. "I have it."

He took the handle to her luggage. "Is it in here?"

"Wait a minute. Mr. Aus..., I mean my associate told me that I'm to give the disk to no one but him. I follow orders."

"I didn't ask you to give it to me. I only asked where it was. But don't get all riled up. I was just trying to make sure we kept it safe. Is it in that tote bag you're carrying?"

Her chin jutted out and her lips curled into a defiant pout. "I don't like your attitude. I've a good mind not to go with you at all."

Cody shrugged and nudged his tan Stetson back on his head. She was a spunky little thing. He guessed it took that to be the kind of woman who'd sell out to the enemy. "If you don't go with me, you might not get paid. And your *associate* would be very upset with both of us. Besides, I have no intention of letting you leave here without me."

"Okay, but don't try to boss me around. You're supposed to protect me and take me to…"

He threw up his hands to stop her babbling. "I'm Cody Gannon and I'm to take you to meet your associate, who we both know is Dan Austin. So let's just get the show on the road."

She took off down the corridor, and he followed, pulling her bag behind him. He slowed to dodge a man with a white cane who was walking against the flow of pedestrian traffic. "My truck is just outside," he said, catching up with her easily.

"I have to stop at baggage claim to get the rest of my luggage. I wasn't sure where I was going so I had to bring sweaters and jackets and everything."

"It's September, Mrs. Rand. You'd have to go a long way to need a suitcase full of sweaters and coats in Texas in September."

"Well, it's *late* September. Anyway, I'm not a Mrs. I was about to tell you that earlier, but you didn't give me a chance to finish." She looked down at her stomach. "The baby's due in late December. I hope it's born for Christmas. I'm keeping my fingers crossed that it's a girl, but I don't want to know until she's born."

She took a deep breath and looked up. It was the first time they'd made real eye contact, and the sudden intimacy of it bothered him. He looked away and walked all the faster.

"I'm sorry," she said, obviously taking his action for disapproval. "When I get nervous, I just can't seem to stop talking. Todd says it's my insecurity. I guess he's probably right.''

''Who's Todd?''

''It doesn't matter.'' She stopped talking and stared straight ahead as they made their way toward the baggage area.

From babbling on and on to complete silence. He hoped she wasn't going to be one of those moody types. One thing for sure, when he agreed to Dan's offer, he hadn't expected that he'd be leading a pregnant woman into a trap that would get her arrested and sent to prison.

Strange, he was supposed to be one of the good guys, but he felt a lot like a rat. He walked beside Sarah to claim her baggage, wishing every second that Dan Austin would call. The sooner he made the delivery and walked away from this, the better he would like it.

''I need to stop at the ladies' room,'' Sarah said. ''Why don't you go on to the baggage area, and I'll meet you there?''

''No way. I was told to stick to you like flies to a Fudgsicle.''

''I don't know why. I came this far. I'm not running out now.''

''I'm just following orders.'' He took her arm and guided her to a spot by the wall where he would be out of the line of traffic but could still see the restroom door. ''When you finish, meet me right here.''

''If you're going to wait on me anyway, you can hold this.'' She thrust the tote bag in his direction.

He grimaced. ''No way. If you want me to hold your bags, you need to buy some that won't get me laughed at.''

''A real cowboy wouldn't let that bother him.'' She set it down at his feet and walked away.

He watched her depart, her hips swaying seductively. Seductively? What in the world was he thinking? You couldn't think words like seductive in reference to a pregnant woman. It was...

He didn't know what it was, but he didn't plan to let it happen again. He touched a finger to the pager at his waist, checking to make sure it was on. All he wanted to do was get this woman and her disk to Daniel Austin.

The disk. Surely it wasn't in the tote bag she'd carelessly deposited at his feet. He yanked it up and started digging through it. A couple of James Bond videos, some books, a portable radio with headphones, an opened package of trail mix, a bottle of vitamins.

Nothing that even resembled a floppy disk or a CD.

He looked up to find a couple of cowboys snickering at his bag. "Don't worry," he quipped. "You're not my type." Before he had time to give it another thought, the pager at his waist vibrated.

He checked the number and then turned to try and locate a pay phone. There was one about thirty yards down the corridor, but he'd have to wait for Sarah before he made the call. Shifting from one foot to the other, he wondered what in the hell was taking her so long.

SOMETHING WAS WRONG. Sarah had known it the second the young cowboy had stepped up and called her by name. Daniel Austin had promised her a bodyguard, and he wouldn't have sent a boy to do a man's job.

Not that the cowboy outside was younger than she was, but he wasn't a heck of a lot older either, and he wasn't big and brawny. He was lean and lank and much too cute and sexy to have ever been in a fight.

She'd become even more suspicious when he'd

started questioning her about the location of the disk. Daniel had warned her that she might run into trouble, that she was not to give the disk to anyone but him. And, if anything alarmed her, she was to sit tight and wait for him to contact her.

That's why she'd made up the story about having a lot of extra baggage. It would have worked, too, if the man waiting outside the ladies' room had agreed to meet her at baggage pickup. Then she could have sneaked away without any problem. Now she'd have to use more desperate methods and pray they worked.

Stopping in front of the mirror, she shrugged her arms into the sleeves of her light coat. It wasn't cold, but it would be easier than carrying it when she made her getaway. Taking a deep breath, she stepped outside the bathroom and walked up behind the cowboy who claimed to be her contact.

"Help, officer. This man stole my bag." Her voice pierced the dull clamor of the crowd, echoing off the walls and ceilings.

Cody grabbed her arm, his fingers digging into her flesh. "What the devil are you doing?"

"Give me my tote bag," she screamed, yanking it from his arm. "Thief."

He grabbed the strap and held on. A crowd gathered around them, and two guys pinned Cody's arms behind him while another pried the bag from his hand and presented it to Sarah. She took off running just as a cop pushed through the circle of onlookers. She didn't wait to see what happened next.

A WALL OF HOT AIR slapped Sarah in the face as she stepped through the double doors and into the hustle of passengers just outside the airport. She had no idea where she should go or what she should do next. Mr. Austin had said she wouldn't need any money. Still, she'd brought all the cash she had on her when he'd called and said it was time to swing into action.

A measly twenty dollars. A cab ride to downtown San Antonio probably cost more than that. Besides, there was no place for her to go once she got downtown. She'd just have to wait until she heard from him. But wait where?

A uniformed police officer stopped traffic and she crossed the street with a group of Japanese tourists headed for a motor van in the outside lane. She left them at the curb, picking up her pace and striding toward the parking garage. She could duck behind a car and wait to hear from Dan.

The dangerous part would be stealing the files, he'd assured her. After that, she could leave everything to him. Only now she was in San Antonio, alone and broke. And hungry. Tears burned at the back of her eyelids. She blinked them away. No one ever cried in James Bond movies. They always managed to do something brave and daring. She made her way to the back corner of the first floor of the garage and crouched behind a white minivan.

Her cellular phone rang, and she dug the phone from her handbag. "Hello."

"Do you have the files, Sarah?"

She recognized Mr. Austin's voice at once, only it wasn't calm the way it usually was. He sounded angry.

"I have them."

"Where are you?"

"I'm in the parking garage at the airport. Your bodyguard didn't show. Instead some cowboy tried to convince me to give him the disk."

"The cowboy you left in the hands of the police *is* the bodyguard. You can trust him to bring you to me, but don't give him the diskette."

"Suppose he takes it away from me?"

"He won't. I've warned him not to upset you any more than he already has. Now, tell me exactly where you are and then stay put until Cody Gannon shows up. He'll bring you to me."

Her voice trembled as she gave her location. Cody Gannon was the last man she wanted to see, but she ended the connection, slipped the phone back into her handbag and waited. The minutes dragged on, and with each one she wished she was back in D.C. in her cozy apartment.

Just her and her baby-to-be.

Footsteps sounded around her. She didn't bother turning around. Cody Gannon would not be glad to see her.

"Waiting for someone, lady?"

The voice was coarse and harsh, not Cody Gannon's. She spun around just as the man's briefcase collided with the side of her head. Her feet slipped and she stumbled awkwardly as her purse was ripped from her arms. She tried to scream, but the man slapped her hard across the face.

Her ears rang and blood spurted from her nose and dripped onto her lips. She tried to brush it away with the back of her hand, but the man grabbed her and pinned her against him, holding his large, meaty hand over her mouth.

He threw her handbag to the hood and ravaged it with his free hand, tossing the contents to the floor. Her cell phone cracked, the pieces went flying into the air and under the minivan. ''If you like living, lady, hand over the disk.''

She'd be glad to, only her fingers wouldn't move and she was seeing two and sometimes three of everything. So she spit into one of the man's faces and let the hot, suffocating blackness consume her as she slumped to the concrete floor.

Chapter Two

Cody raced across the busy street and ducked inside the doors of the parking garage. Dan had chewed him out good for letting Sarah outsmart him, but his stinging comments hadn't been nearly as caustic as the ones Cody had hurled at himself.

He'd had a hell of a time convincing the cop that he and Sarah had just had a lover's quarrel and that causing the scene was her way of getting back at him. He doubted the cop believed him, but he'd released him anyway, thanks to the testimony of a middle-aged woman who claimed to have witnessed the whole show.

When he found Sarah, he would tell her how the cow ate the cabbage and he wouldn't mince words doing it. He was delivering her to Austin if he had to handcuff her and tie her to the truck. Pregnant or not, she was a little spitfire, and he'd have no choice but to treat her like one.

He rushed past a man carrying a briefcase in one hand and an overstuffed duffel in the other as he made his way to the back of the parking garage. Someone's alarm went off. He barely noticed. Dan had said Sarah would be waiting for him near the left back corner, behind a minivan. This was the first time Cody realized how many people drove minivans.

"Sarah." He said her name, too softly to attract any undue attention, but loudly enough she could hear him if she were within a few yards. There was no answer. He kept walking. He was almost to the back corner now, and there was no one around. Nothing but parked cars and exhaust fumes wafting on the humid air.

And a moan.

Anxiety and a burst of adrenaline answered. He called her name again and tried to follow the direction of the sound. A large man in a dark shirt and jeans dashed from between a car and a white minivan, then disappeared behind a Land Cruiser.

Cody's first instinct was to take off after the guy, but his job was finding the woman. He sprinted the last few feet, reaching the minivan in record time. And there he found Sarah Rand, on the floor, her back slumped against the fender.

The sight ground like raw hamburger in his stomach. Her hot pink suit was sprayed with blood that dripped from her red nose. Her eyes were open, but glazed and unfocused. The contents of her purse were scattered around her. And a knot was rising on the side of her head.

The anger he'd felt toward her a minute ago was swallowed by a wave of compassion that overrode his determination to treat her as the criminal she was. Reaching into his back pocket, he pulled out a thankfully clean handkerchief and held it to her nose to catch the drops of crimson blood. "What happened?"

"Like you care."

"If I didn't care, I wouldn't have asked. Besides, I'm getting paid to care."

"Some brute was trying to steal the disk. He sneaked up on me and hit me in the head. When I tried to fight him off he slapped me in the face and almost knocked my lights out."

Dropping to his knees, he brushed stray locks of hair from her face. "Are you all right?"

"Is my head still attached?"

"It's still there." As gingerly as he could, he touched his fingertips to the knot just above her right ear. "In fact it looks as if you're growing another one."

"And both of them hurt." She put her weight on her hands and pushed against the van, helping herself to a standing position. She staggered, and he stepped in to steady her.

"I think you should see a doctor," he said, holding her unsteady body against his.

"Not for a knot on the head."

"You could have a concussion."

"I could have, but I don't. I'm a little disoriented, but my vision is okay now. And I'm not nauseous."

"I still think you should see a doctor. We can stop in at an emergency room. Hopefully, we can make up some story that won't require alerting the police."

"I told you I'm fine." She touched her hand to the swell beneath her dress. "Nothing important hurts. But, believe me, if I start having pains in my stomach, I'll let you know. I won't take chances with my baby."

"No use taking chances with a concussion either."

"If I develop the symptoms of a concussion, I'll seek medical help. Trust me."

Trust her? Not in this life, not with the credentials she carried. Still, he planned to deliver her alive and in reasonably good condition. "How do you know so much about the symptoms of concussions? Do you make a habit of getting attacked by strangers?''

''My mother was a nurse, a very good one. She practically ran the hospital where she worked. She taught me all about first aid for trauma.''

Yeah, well, Cody had learned a lot about first aid from his mother, too. Only she hadn't been a nurse. She'd been a victim—a lot more times than he cared to think about. He waited until Sarah was steady on her feet before he asked the big question. ''Did the man who attacked you get the disk?''

She closed her eyes and then opened them slowly, leveling him with a cold stare. ''That's all you people care about. You and Mr. Austin. I'm just a pawn to you.''

''You're a pawn. I'm a pawn. The brute who hit you over the head is probably a pawn, too. Just not one of ours.''

It was a stupid answer. Sarah Rand wasn't a pawn to him. She was less than that. She was a traitorous mercenary. So why had he come to her rescue instead of going after the brute?

''He didn't get the disk,'' she said.

Relief settled in Cody's chest, like a cool breath on a hot day. ''Maybe he wasn't after the disk at all. Maybe he really was a purse snatcher.'' He stooped and started picking up the jumble of makeup and papers that had been emptied from her bag.

''No, it was the disk he wanted. He threatened to kill me if I didn't give it to him.''

''So much for wishing for a simple purse snatching.''

''Simple for you. You're not the one who took a briefcase to the side of your head.''

Cody scooped up the last of the items and stuffed

them into the open handbag. "You wouldn't have either if you hadn't pulled that stunt in the airport. We'd have been in my pickup on the way to collect your payoff."

"A pickup truck?"

"What did you expect? A Rolls?"

"I guess I should be thankful you didn't ride in on your horse."

"According to your tote bag, the one you accused me of stealing, that would have suited you just fine."

"The bag was a gift," she said. "From someone with a bizarre sense of humor."

"Imagine you having bizarre friends. But enough friendly chitchat. We need to get on our way. Is it the emergency room or the highway?" Cody asked, scanning the area for any sign of more trouble.

"The highway." She ran her hands down her skirt, smoothing the wrinkles but avoiding the bloodstains. "I'm almost back to normal now, and I'd like to get this over with as soon as possible."

"I'm sure you would." Get it over with and collect one million dollars in cold, hard cash. He picked up her tote bag and grabbed the handle of her luggage. She pulled her coat over her shoulders and walked a few steps before stopping to wait on him.

He watched her to make sure she wasn't lying about feeling normal. Her nose had quit bleeding, and she was steady on her feet. But she still looked like a little girl playing grown-up in her hot pink maternity clothes.

No matter that he didn't like her value system, he couldn't deny that she was attractive, in a girl-next-door sort of way. The look probably served her well, kept anyone from suspecting her of wrongdoing. She was probably the darling of the Washington office where she worked.

But she wouldn't be able to smile and charm her way out of the trouble she was in now. A trap had been set, and she was following the bait right through the cage door.

Only, apparently Dan wasn't the only one who knew she had the disk. The guy who'd nearly taken her head off had known it, too. Only how did he know and who was he? Had Calderone outsmarted everyone again? Had he found out what Dan was up to and decided to send one of his own men after the disk?

If so, Dan Austin was in big trouble. They all were.

SARAH STARED out the window. The late afternoon sky was bordered by a band of gold that gilded the rolling hills. Cows, horses, fences, all far different from what she was used to seeing on her morning commute.

She really didn't mind riding in a pickup truck. In fact, she liked it. She just wasn't about to admit it to the cocky cowboy behind the wheel.

The same way she hadn't admitted that she'd bought the tote because she'd always fantasized about falling in love with a cowboy and having him fall right back in love with her. Now she was with a cowboy, and it wasn't nearly as exciting as she'd imagined. The cowboy in question hadn't seemed to notice that she was a woman. Still that was probably better than filling her head with lies the way Todd Benson had done.

She settled back in her seat and took a sip of the milk Cody had bought for her when he'd stopped at the convenience store for ice for her injury. Turning her head, she studied the rugged lines of Cody's profile. He looked intense, as if his mind were a billion miles away from here. And he was much too quiet. It made her nervous.

She squirmed in her seat. "If Dan hasn't told you where to meet him, how do you know we're going in the right direction?"

"He said to take Highway 281 north and to stay on it until we hear from him—unless I spot someone following us."

"You mean like the man who attacked me at the airport."

He turned her way for a second before returning his gaze to the road. "I hope you're not doing anything really stupid, like trying to set Dan up."

"Of course not. What kind of woman do you think I am?"

"How would I know what kind of woman you are? We just met."

"I'm trying to help. That's all."

They settled into a strained silence. Apparently he was still angry that she'd run from him back at the airport, but he could just get over it. They were in this together. They might as well make the most of it. And she hated to ride in silence. Better to ask questions and force him to talk. "Are you married?"

His face twisted into a scowl. "No way."

"You don't have to bite my head off. I was just thinking that it must be rough to leave your wife at home when you go off on one of these missions. If you had one."

"That's why I don't. What about you? Why didn't you marry that Todd guy you were talking about?"

"Todd didn't want me. Well, actually, he did want *me*. He didn't want *our* child. He thought I should, you know, get rid of it or at least give it up for adoption."

"But you wanted to keep your baby?"

Wanted. The word was probably accurate, but it

seemed so mild compared to the feelings that had come over her from the second the pregnancy test had come back positive. It wasn't that she was against adoption. She knew there were many wonderful people out there who ached for a baby of their own and couldn't have one, people who could give the baby a good home.

But the baby growing inside her was wanted by its biological mother. Wanted and needed. And already loved. "There is no way I'm giving up my baby."

"So Todd just took off and left you stranded?"

"Something like that."

"He isn't the first man to walk away and leave an expectant mother to shift for herself. Guess fatherhood puts too much of a damper on some men's lifestyles."

Sarah had the strange feeling that Cody was no longer talking about her at all. His tone had taken on an intensity that seemed too personal for conversation between strangers.

But then nothing about their being together was normal.

"Were you in love with Todd?"

The question took her by surprise. If he'd asked her three months ago, the answer would have been an unqualified yes. "I thought I was at the time. Now I think I was only in love with being in love. A woman dreams of that all her life. Romance. The perfect man. I mean, songs, poems, movies—they're all about falling in love."

"So what changed your mind?"

"I expected to fall apart when he left. I didn't. The truth was my life got easier with no one around to tell me that I couldn't do anything on my own. Two years of hearing that constantly and you start to believe it."

"Wait a minute. Are you saying you dated this guy

for two years and then he just walked out of your life because you were pregnant with his baby?''

"Two years and three months to be exact. He counted it up for me when he left, just in case I couldn't.''

"You must have been a teenager when you started dating him.''

"I'm a lot older than I look, twenty-seven on my next birthday. But Todd was my first serious beau.''

"Looks like waiting around didn't improve your judgment.''

"I wasn't exactly waiting around. My life was too busy to think of relationships before that. I worked my way through university, taking night classes until I could earn my degree in business.''

"Didn't your mother help you pay for your education?''

"My mother?''

"Yeah, you know, your wonderful nurse mother who practically runs the hospital.''

She turned to stare out the window. "She wanted to, but she had quit her job at the hospital by then to do missionary work in Africa.''

"She sounds like quite a woman.''

"She is.''

Cody reached down and checked the beeper at his waist. "Looks like Dan is ready for us. Too bad your cell phone got destroyed in the attack.''

"Don't you have one?''

"Not anymore.''

"What will you do?''

"Find a pay phone somewhere.''

"Last minute directions. Secret destinations.'' She

stretched her legs in front of her. "This is awfully intriguing, don't you think?"

"I never thought of it like that."

"That's because you're a cowboy who's merely serving as a guide and bodyguard. You don't have a full understanding or appreciation for the importance of this mission."

He glanced her way and rolled his eyes. "No, ma'am. I'm just an ignorant cowboy at your service."

He was making fun of her now. She'd never been able to pull off that sophisticated routine. But, this was exciting, whether Cody Gannon wanted to admit it or not. Living on the edge. Doing something important. She'd waited for this moment all her life. Too bad that Cody was the only one around to see her, and he apparently wasn't impressed.

And too bad reality reared its ugly head every so often and reminded her what would happen if anything went wrong with this operation. Only nothing would go wrong. Dan Austin was one of the best agents the DPS had ever had.

They drove another ten minutes until they came to a gas station. Cody pulled off and parked near the phone booth. "I'll only be a minute." He killed the engine and yanked his keys from the ignition.

"I didn't plan to leave you," she said, as he jumped out of the truck, dangling the key ring from his fingers.

"I'm not taking any chances. Not with my truck."

She stuck her tongue out at him. A not-at-all sophisticated thing to do, but he was way too cocky.

She watched as he deposited his money and punched in the number. His mouth moved, so he was talking to someone, but his scowl indicated he was not happy with the call. After a minute or two, he slammed the receiver into its cradle and climbed back behind the steering wheel.

"Did Dan tell you where we're supposed to meet him?"

"Yeah."

"You don't sound as if you like it."

"Driving into Mexico with a pregnant woman is not my idea of fun, especially when we've spent the last two hours driving in the opposite direction."

Without warning, her stomach turned inside out. "I didn't bargain for going into Mexico."

"You can always back out," he said.

And if she didn't know better, she'd think that was what he wanted her to do. But that wouldn't make sense. He worked for Mr. Austin. "I won't back out. I always keep my word. But I might pass out if we don't stop for dinner soon."

"Then dinner it is. Better to give the devil his due on a full stomach."

"You know, Cody Gannon, half the time I don't have a clue what you're talking about."

"Then we should make a good pair, because I don't have a clue what I'm doing here."

He swerved out of the parking lot and onto the road. "The rest of the ride may be a little bumpy."

"Why?"

"Look behind you."

She did. "I see a highway, passing fence posts, and there's some horses in that field we just passed."

"There's a blue car back there somewhere, too. He's been with us for the past fifteen miles or so. When I slow down, he slows down."

"So that's why we've been racing along half the time

and crawling the other half? Do you think it's the man who attacked me at the airport?''

''Whoever it is, I plan to lose him. So make sure your seat belt's buckled.''

She checked the buckle, excitement dancing along her nerve endings. A cute cowboy, a secret mission, and someone following them. If this were a movie, the action music would start up right now.

THE RESTAURANT where they stopped was little more than a clapboard shell with a roof, but the parking lot was crowded. New and old cars and several pickup trucks jammed into the narrow space in front of the building, and that was always a good sign. Eat where the locals chow down and you can't go wrong.

Cody opened the door for Sarah and helped her out of the truck. She planted her feet on the cracked asphalt and then reached back for her coat.

''I don't think you'll need that.''

''Not for warmth, but if you think I'm going in there sporting bloodstains, you've got another think coming.''

''Well, *excuuuse* me. If I'd known I was dining with a fashion plate, I'd have wiped the dust off my boots. But I can tell you without walking in the door that no one in this place is going to get all bent out of shape over a couple of stains.''

''Nonetheless, I'll wear my wrap. My mother always says that if you want to be treated like a lady, you should look and act like one.''

''Then I'm glad your mother wasn't there to watch your performance in the airport.'' But still he held her coat while she slid her arms into the sleeves.

Her hair brushed his fingers. The softness of the

strands contrasted with the rough texture of the coat, and he jerked his hands away. She might look and act and even feel like a lady, but she wasn't one. She was just another criminal playing innocent, and he was way too smart to fall for her act.

He opened the door to the restaurant and was greeted by an assault of odors and a sudden attack of home-sickness. The peppers, the onions, the smell of freshly baked tortillas. It was like walking into Rosa's kitchen back at the Smoking Barrel. Only it wasn't his buddies sitting around the table but a room full of strangers.

A waitress with a tray laden with sizzling fajitas sa-shayed by them. "Welcome to Carmelita's," she said, flashing them a smile. "Sit where you like. I think there's still some empty tables in the back."

Sarah made her way through the maze of tables and mismatched chairs without waiting for him. He fol-lowed along behind, glancing about the room as he did. The place looked safe enough, mostly families and a few young guys still sporting ranch dust on their faded jeans. A pudgy woman in a flowered dress caught him staring her way and smiled. He smiled back.

All well and good. Not that he expected trouble in here. He'd watched his tail ever since they'd left the gas station, cut through a field and down a deserted road before pulling out on this highway. But the attack back at the airport had him spooked. And the first thing he'd learned from Mitchell Forbes had been to never let his guard down.

He'd made a mistake back at the airport, but he didn't plan to make any more.

Sarah had already pulled out her own chair and taken a seat by the time he caught up with her. "Didn't your mother tell you that a lady waits for a man to hold her chair?''

''I'm perfectly capable of doing that for myself.''

''Still, it makes me look bad.''

''I didn't know you were into playing the gentleman.''

''A real cowboy doesn't *play* at being a gentleman. It comes naturally.''

''Do tell. Then I may have to reconsider my opinion of the saying on my tote bag. I'm not used to dining with a gentleman.''

''I take it Todd wasn't one.''

''He probably was in the beginning. You know how it is after you date the same person for a long time.''

''No, can't say that I do. Not unless four or five dates qualifies as a long time.''

''Four or five dates? You could do that in a week.''

''Maybe *you* could. Ranching hours don't lend themselves to that kind of courting, especially when the ranch is five miles past the end of the world.''

''So why aren't you out on the edge of nowhere punching cattle tonight, Cody Gannon, instead of taxiing me around?''

The answer was simple enough, but he kept it to himself. He wasn't punching cattle because he no longer had a job. He didn't belong on the Smoking Barrel anymore. He didn't belong anywhere, and even if he had, he wouldn't be at liberty to discuss it with Sarah.

If she had any idea that he was one of the good guys, that this was a trap, she'd run like a hellion at the first opportunity, maybe even destroy the disk completely. Or worse yet, actually get it to Calderone.

The waitress set a basket of greasy chips and a white

crockery bowl of salsa in the center of the table. "Watch that stuff," she said, tapping a painted fingernail on the edge of the bowl. "It's hotter than a honeymoon hotel." She laughed at her own joke and then pulled a pencil and order pad from her apron pocket. "What can I get you folks? Everything on the menu's good and the bartender makes a great margarita."

"I'll take a beer," Cody said. "Whatever you have on tap, as long as it's cold. Maybe the lady would like a margarita."

"Indeed not." Sarah stared at him as if he'd committed a cardinal sin. "Alcohol is strictly off-limits for pregnant women. Haven't you read the warnings? They're posted on the bathroom door of every ladies' room in the country."

"Sorry. I don't spend a lot of time hanging out in ladies' rooms. But I wasn't trying to force a drink on you. It was just a suggestion. Drink and eat whatever you like."

"Are you paying?"

"Sure. Why not?" She was awful tight for a woman who was about to collect more money than he'd probably accumulate in a lifetime. At least she thought she was about to get paid.

Of course, she might be busted, and if she really was hard up for cash, that might explain why she'd sold out to the enemy. An unmarried woman about to have a baby could probably feel pretty desperate if she didn't have the money for medical expenses and diapers and such.

He listened while Sarah placed her order and then gave the waitress his, surprised to find that he was actually hungry. Rosa had accused him more than once of eating anything that didn't eat him first, but since

he'd left the Smoking Barrel, he'd lost his taste for
food. At least working again gave him an appetite even
if he didn't take to the job. It had one pregnant woman
too many for his liking.

As soon as the waitress walked away, Sarah dived
into the chips, dipping one into the salsa before slipping
it between her lips. "I absolutely love Mexican food.
Don't you?"

"I like it well enough."

Sarah nibbled on another chip. "Actually I love anything hot and spicy. The first three months I was pregnant I got sick every time I ate a bite of food with a
little zip to it. It drove me nuts. But now I can eat
anything without getting sick. Well, most of the time
anyway."

A few minutes, and a couple of thousand words later,
the waitress returned with their food and drinks. He ate
and half listened to Sarah's chatter. If she kept this up
all the way to Mexico, he'd have to seriously consider
gagging her or at least stuffing cotton in his ears. If
they actually went to Mexico. He needed more reason
to believe this whole operation was on the up-and-up
before he sealed this deal.

"Have you ever been afraid, Cody?"

He looked up and met her gaze, wondering where
the question had come from and when her tone had
changed from light to deadly serious. "Not lately."

"But you have been at some time in your life?"

Old memories surfaced. He pushed them aside, back
into the dead file where he'd buried them long ago. "I
imagine everybody's been scared of something at one
time or another."

"I'm scared now. Excited, but still scared, especially

when I stop to think about what would happen if something went wrong.''

Her voice caught, and a protectiveness he didn't want to acknowledge rattled inside him. ''No one's making you go through with this, Sarah.''

''You have a short memory, Cody. You said you wouldn't let me out of your sight until you'd delivered me and the disk to Daniel Austin.''

He swallowed hard. He'd made a lot of mistakes in his life, but that's all they'd been. Mistakes in judgment. He'd never jumped sides, never played on the team that wore the black hats. Yet here he was, aching to give comfort and solace to the enemy.

And all because the bad guy was a woman. A scared, young pregnant woman. ''I'm just doing my job, Sarah.''

''I know. I guess we're all just doing what we have to do. I don't want to change anything. But, all the same, I'm a little scared.''

Silence grew thick and suffocating between them. He pushed his plate away, his appetite lost to an unexplained regret that had crept into his gut.

A few minutes later, he paid the bill and they left the restaurant, the silence still holding between them. And strange as it seemed, he missed her chatter.

SARAH WINCED, trying to bite back the groan that hung in her throat. She'd bragged about being able to eat anything, but Carmelita's enchilada platter had proven her wrong. Her chest burned as if she'd swallowed fire, and her stomach was turning itself inside out.

She closed her eyes as a new wave of nausea washed

over her. Cody turned his gaze from the road to her.
"Is something wrong?"

"Just a little upset stomach. I'll be fine."

"You don't look fine." Cody reached up and flicked
on the inside light, knocking the edge off the grayness
of dusk. "You look like you saw a ghost."

"It's nothing. I just get pale when I feel queasy."

"You're not about to do anything drastic are you?
We're a long way from a hospital."

"Drastic?"

"You know, like have a baby."

"No, cowboy. But maybe you better pull over for a
minute. I might do something drastic like lose my dinner."

He pulled over, only now he looked a little pale himself. Obviously he wasn't used to tending a sick
woman. He stopped the truck and jumped out, rushing
around the truck to open her door.

"Try to breathe a little fresh air. Maybe that will
help."

She cradled her head in her hands. "Do we have
much farther to go?"

"Half the night."

She groaned.

Cody hunched down beside her. "Look, we don't
have to rush. Daniel's the one who had us waste time
driving in the opposite direction. He can just bide his
time until you feel like traveling."

"Thanks." His concern surprised her. Todd had
hated it when she first started waking up with morning
sickness, always finding a reason why he couldn't stay
around, until the morning he'd just walked off for good.

"We can sit here as long as you need to. There's no
rush."

"It's all right, Cody. I can make it," she assured him. "I just needed to stop for a minute. I feel better now."

"Like hell you do." He took her hand. "I don't know much about having a baby, but I know when a woman's hurting. You need to see a doctor, and I plan to find you one."

"No. I have something to take." She unzipped her purse and located the small bottle of antacid tablets. "A couple of these and I'll be good as new."

"You had a blow to the head earlier today. Now you're nauseous. We're seeing a doctor."

"Dan won't like that."

"That's just too bad."

"I have a better idea."

"We're not calling your mother in Africa."

"That wasn't my idea. I was going to suggest calling my gynecologist in Washington. Dr. Marino knows my history and he knows how my stomach reacts to spicy food. If he thinks I should see a doctor, I'll follow his advice."

"Okay, but even if he says you don't need to see a doctor, I'm finding a place for us to stay tonight. Tomorrow we'll get up early and drive into Mexico. That makes more sense anyway."

"Then you'll have to get two rooms."

"Why?"

"I can't sleep with you."

He dropped her hand. "Nice try, Miss Rand, but you and I are going to be real close tonight. I don't buy your innocent gambit."

She shuddered. "What does that mean?"

"That I have no intention of giving you the chance to run out on me like you did at the airport. I'll be right beside you all night long, but you don't need to worry about your virtue with me. I'm choosy about who I take to bed.''

She swung her legs back into the truck and folded her hands over her bulging stomach, suddenly aware of how her misshapen body must look to him. She'd have laughed out loud if she didn't feel so bad.

Still, it would be her first time to spend a night with a cowboy. Maybe there was some kind of charm attached to carrying that tote bag.

Chapter Three

A half hour later Cody turned off the nearly deserted asphalt road and pulled onto a completely deserted dirt one. It was too dark to see anything except sporadic clusters of brush that bordered the road and an occasional stubby tree.

The antacid tablets had eased the stomach discomfort and her head no longer ached from the blow she'd received earlier that day. She was tough, always had been. It was only her petite size that fooled people, but she couldn't deny that a bed would feel really good about now. They hit a hole, and she grabbed hold of the armrest to keep from falling over onto Cody. "Is this the most desolate place you can find?"

"On short notice."

Apprehension set her stomach rolling again. "You said we were going to look for a place to spend the night. You surely don't expect to find a motel down this lousy excuse for a road."

"Not a motel, but the sign back there said there's a fishing camp down here with rustic cabins."

"I don't doubt the rustic part."

"It won't be the Holiday Inn, but we shouldn't have to worry about anyone finding us down here."

"That sounds as if you think someone is still looking."

"I haven't spotted anyone who looked even vaguely suspicious since we left the restaurant, but I don't take chances unless I have to."

She put her hand to her mouth, almost catching the end of her fingernail between her teeth before she jerked it away. It was no time to show weakness. "Mr. Austin failed to mention that delivery of the files would be this dangerous."

"Would it have made a difference?"

She considered the question. "It might have. I wouldn't have worried about myself so much, but I have my unborn child to consider."

"Now's a fine time to think about that."

His attitude annoyed her. "Don't you ever take risks, Cody Gannon?"

"All the time." He nudged his Stetson back a notch, and a sprinkling of dark, wavy hair peeked out from under the edge of the hat. "I just don't want tonight to be one of them."

"That makes two of us."

SARAH LEANED against the doorframe of the small office while Cody registered them as Mr. and Mrs. Carpenter. He paid the bill for one night's lodging in advance—in cash.

She lost track of the conversation, as the middle-aged woman who'd introduced herself as the owner drawled on, more nosy than she had a right to be. Instead Sarah shuffled through memories, searching for something pleasant to latch on to.

A morning five months ago when she'd stood in Dr. Marino's office and he'd told her that the test she'd taken at home had been accurate. She was carrying a new life inside her. The events that followed played in her mind, turning sour when she got to the point where she delivered the news to Todd.

"You don't look so good."

She jumped at the voice. The woman had walked over to stand beside her. "I ate some spicy food," Sarah answered, looking away from the woman's appraising stare. "I took a couple of antacid tablets. I'll be fine. I just need a bed."

"Hmmmph. I'd say you need a sight more than that." The woman's gaze traveled from Sarah's swollen nose to the dried bloodstain on the front of her clothes. Then she looked back at Cody, disgust twisting her mouth and narrowing her eyes.

It took Sarah a few seconds to decipher her meaning. The woman believed that Cody had hit her. "This isn't what it seems," Sarah assured her and then wondered why she bothered. It was clear from the woman's patronizing smile that she didn't believe her.

The woman laid a hand on Sarah's shoulder. "I'll be working until nine. If you need anything, just call me." Her gaze shifted to Cody and then back again. "And you don't have to put up with anything as long as you're staying in one of my cabins. I have a night watchman on duty. He's tough as a wild coyote. Nobody scares him."

Sarah looked up to find Cody doing his own impression of a big, tough Texan behind the woman's back. Any other time, she'd have had to laugh. Even now, she managed a smile. "If I need you, or the night watchman, I'll definitely call."

The woman stood in the door and watched them as they left the office and walked back to the truck. The cabin she'd assigned them was at the end of the road, set off by itself.

"That's the first time I've been accused of being a wife beater," Cody said, as he took her elbow and guided her around a rut in the path.

"She didn't accuse you."

"Oh, no? If looks could kill, I'd be waiting on morgue pick-up right now."

"As it is, you better walk a thin, straight line or I'll have her sic the night watchman on you."

"She's probably calling him right now, to put him on alert so he can start flexing his big, tough muscles. Of course, once he finds out its a looker he's to protect, he might flex a new muscle. Then you'd be wishing you had me back."

"Or maybe not. I haven't seen the big, tough watchman yet." But his comment stayed with her. Cody saw her as attractive. Interesting, especially since most of the time he treated her as if she had something contagious.

The night watchman stepped into the clearing surrounding the office just as they reached the truck. The woman hadn't lied. The man was big, at least a head taller than Cody with muscles a body builder would have envied. A gun rested in a holster at his waist but it was the chainsaw he held in his hand that sent shivers up Sarah's spine.

"It's almost dark. Why would he be chopping down trees this time of night?" she asked.

Cody opened the truck door for her. "He's probably cutting some logs into firewood."

"Hmm. Does chainsaw massacre have any meaning for you?"

"It didn't. It does now." He touched a hand to her

arm. "But don't worry. You have a cowboy to protect you. You know, so many cowboys, so little time."

"You against the machismo guard dog. Now I feel so much better."

SARAH STEPPED inside the cabin. It was one room, with a sink, range, table and four chairs on one end and a bed, chest and upholstered chair on the other. An open door led to a closet-sized bathroom. The mattress was lumpy, narrow, topped with a faded spread and two pillows that had lost their fluff years ago. Still, it had been an extremely long and eventful day, and she couldn't remember when a bed had looked so inviting.

Cody reached to take her coat from around her shoulders. She held on to it for a second, then relinquished it. If she made too much of a fuss, he'd figure out why she never let it out of her sight.

Cody hung up the coat and then walked over to stand beside her. "Now that we've settled for the night, you should give your doctor a call."

"If it will make you happy. But I'm fine." She called the after-hours number and left a message for her gynecologist to call her back. Then she slipped out of her shoes and stretched out on the bed. "My mother always said that the best thing for a queasy stomach is to lie very still and think pleasant thoughts."

"Yeah, well my mother always gave me a cold, wet cloth for my head. We weren't big on pleasant thoughts around my house."

He walked away and came back a few moments later with a damp cloth. The bed shifted as he sat down on the edge of it and pressed the thin washcloth against her forehead. She stared up at him, studying his expression. The worry was evident. She wondered if it was really for her.

"Why don't you crawl under the covers and get comfortable," he said. "If you need anything, I'll be right here."

"That's the nicest thing you've said since you met me at the airport." She closed her eyes. Actually, promising to be there for her might be the nicest thing anyone had ever said to her, she decided, as she took his suggestion and snuggled between the sheets.

Too bad the emotion stemmed from the fact that he was being paid to deliver her and the disk. Both of them had to be kept safe and sound until they were turned over to Daniel Austin. Then his duties would be fulfilled, and he'd no longer be there if she needed anything.

Neither would anyone else.

CODY PACED the motel room. The air conditioner hadn't stopped running since they'd come in, nearly an hour ago, but still the air was sultry and suffocating. He hated being cooped up in this one-room cabin, hated more that this operation had gone wrong. Beginning with the moment Sarah Rand had stepped off that airplane—pregnant.

He glanced at her sleeping form, her blond hair all mussed and spreading over the pillow, the rounding of her stomach beneath the sheets. The cloth he'd given her had been tossed aside, the corner of it dangling from the edge of the honey-colored nightstand. He picked it up and carried it into the cubbyhole of a bathroom.

A cold, wet cloth. That was the extent of what he knew about tending an upset stomach. Sarah, on the other hand, appeared to know what to do for every ailment. From bumps on the head to indigestion, she was a walking medical encyclopedia.

Amazingly enough, Dr. Marino had backed her up when he'd called, said that if she was having no further complications, rest was probably the best thing for her. But, if she became sick to her stomach again or developed a lasting headache, she was to see a doctor at once.

A rectangle of fading light found its way through the narrow window at the back of the cabin and caught Sarah in its glow. Cody stared at her for a minute, then swallowed hard. The woman might look all sweet and innocent when she was asleep, but the images were totally deceptive. She was a woman willing to sell out to the devil himself for cold hard cash.

And if ever there was a devil walking around in a man's body it was Tomaso Calderone. Murdering innocent people came as easily to him as swatting a mosquito did to most folks. Only he seldom did the killing himself. He paraded around his palatial estate wearing designer clothes and partying with a bevy of beautiful women while his paid assassins did whatever it took to keep the drugs rolling into the States and the money rolling into his bank account.

Anything for money. Calderone and Sarah Rand had a lot in common.

The pager at his waist vibrated. He pulled it loose and cradled it in his hand while he checked the number. More bad luck. It was the number to the office phone at the Smoking Barrel.

He crossed the room and stopped at the window. It looked out on the back of the building. A narrow river meandered a few yards away. Beyond that, the land stretched into thorny brush, a few scrubby trees and a line of ever-present barbwire.

Moonlight painted them in shadows and whispers of silver, a magical touch that contradicted the ruggedness of the land. He'd lived in Texas all his life, wandered from one part to the other, found work where he could, staying in one place only until the need to move on would hit again. That had never taken long, not until he'd arrived at the Smoking Barrel.

He exhaled sharply and moved away from the window. The Smoking Barrel was part of his past. It held nothing for him and he had no desire to hear anything Mitchell Forbes had to say. He hoped the man didn't hold his breath waiting for him to return the page.

Determined and weary, he strode back to the door. He needed to move the truck out of sight, park it beyond the patch of thick brush. His job was to keep Sarah Rand safe until the disk was delivered into Daniel's hand, and he never quit on a job until it was finished. But once it was, he planned to get as far away from Texas and the Smoking Barrel as he could.

Montana sounded good to him. So did Alaska.

Muscles tight and drawn, he opened the door. It creaked and groaned, but Sarah didn't move a muscle. Just as well. This might be the last night she slept in a bed without bars around it.

The thought burned in his brain and pulverized his will. He wanted to see Calderone brought down more than he'd ever wanted anything in his life, but he hadn't bargained for this.

"CODY."

He jumped, his head flying from the back of the chair

as he reached for the lamp switch. "What's wrong?" The grogginess of sleep cracked his voice.

"I'm sorry. I didn't mean to wake you. I just wondered if you were still here."

"I'm here." He pushed up his sleeve and checked his watch. Only eleven-thirty, but it seemed much later. "How are you feeling?"

"Good. I told you all I needed was some rest. Getting out of that bouncing truck didn't hurt either." She pushed up on her elbows. The sheet fell from her shoulders, and he realized with a jolt that between the time he'd fallen asleep and now, she'd crawled out of most of her clothes, including her bra. The silky border of her slip dipped low, and her nipples were outlined against the revealing fabric.

She's not only pregnant with another man's baby but she's a rotten mercenary, he reminded himself, hoping his body was listening.

Apparently noticing the direction of his gaze, Sarah grabbed the sheet and pulled it up to her neck. "How well do you know Daniel Austin, Cody?"

"Well enough."

"That's a nonstatement if I ever heard one. What did he tell you about me?"

"Not much." Not that she was pregnant or that she was almost as good at disguises as Dan himself. Her ability to appear innocent was messing with his mind and he knew better. "He said you were bringing some files that he wanted and that I was to make sure you and the disk arrived safely."

"Why didn't he meet me at the airport himself?"

"I couldn't say."

She sat up straight and stared at him, her pink lips

all pouty. "I just don't get it, Cody. Are you always this curt, or do you just not like me?"

Cody hesitated. Any answer he gave would have to be an out-and-out lie or else give too much away. She had to believe that both he and Austin were working for Calderone now.

"It's the situation that's making me edgy," he finally answered. "Not you." He walked to the sink for a glass of water. On second thought, he filled two of the glasses with water from the tap. He walked back to the bed and handed one to Sarah.

"Is this a peace offering?" she asked, taking the glass from his hands.

"You could call it that."

"Then I accept."

She drank heartily, no sissy sipping. If he'd met her anywhere else but under the present circumstances, he'd have sworn she didn't possess an ounce of pretense. But then he would have sworn the same about Mitchell Forbes before he found out differently.

"So tell me, Sarah, what do you plan to do once you deliver the disk to Daniel Austin?"

"Go back to work and save all the money I can. I have insurance to pay the hospital and doctor expenses, but I want to stay home for at least six months so that I can bond with my child. I think that's important, don't you? I mean those early months are crucial in an infant's development."

"I don't know much about infants," he admitted. "But it makes sense that a baby would like to have its own mother around while he's adjusting to the world. I doubt my mother had that option, though, and I grew up just fine."

"You grew up kind of grouchy," she corrected him,

"with a serious lack of social skills. Anyway, you said *he,* and I think my baby's a girl."

"Is that what your doctor said?"

"No, but I'm good at predicting things. You know, it's like I see them before they happen. And every time I think of my baby, I picture her dressed in a dainty pink dress with little pink booties and a lacy bonnet. In fact, I'm so sure that I already bought the bonnet."

Cody turned away. He was seeing things, too, and they stuck in his throat so that he could barely swallow. The image was of Sarah in a prison-gray uniform, her shiny blond hair cut short and stuffed under a cap while she slaved away in a prison laundry. But she must really take him for a fool, talking about saving money when she'd struck a million-dollar deal with Dan.

He swung back to face her. She was smoothing the sheet over her stomach, looking at the bulge as if it were some treasure she'd just discovered. Sweat beaded on his forehead, even though the room had finally cooled. This pregnancy thing was getting to him.

His pager vibrated. He grabbed it, thankful that this time it was not the Smoking Barrel's number that appeared on the screen. Grabbing the phone, he punched in the number.

"Where are you?" Daniel asked, not bothering with small talk or even a hello.

"At a fishing camp just outside of Blanco."

"Blanco? What in the hell are you doing there?"

"We stopped for dinner, and the enchiladas made Sarah sick. I had to find a place for her to get some R-and-R."

"The woman gets an upset stomach, and you find her a bed. How sweet."

"Save the sarcasm, Austin. If you wanted this done differently, you should have done it yourself."

"I had other matters to attend to. Just remember that there is no margin for error in this operation, Cody. None. *Nada*. So don't start mollycoddling the dame, and don't fall for any of her tricks."

"I'm not falling for anything. And if you're so concerned about the success of this operation, why didn't you level with me from the beginning?"

"I have no idea what you're talking about."

"Then let's start with your failure to mention that Sarah Rand was pregnant or to tell me that someone else might know she had the disk."

"I told you everything you needed to know. Now I'm telling you to get out of that cabin and hightail it to Nuevo Laredo. I'm waiting on you."

"Yeah, well I don't hightail so well on back roads, but we'll clear out of here just before daybreak, after Sarah's had a good night's rest."

"You know how important this is, Cody. We've let Calderone slip through our hands too many times. If Sarah is the source of the DPS's leak, we have to stop her."

"And where does Mitchell Forbes fit into this?"

"Sarah isn't the only one Calderone is using. It looks like he was also in tight with her ex-boss, Grover Rucker, and everyone knows Grover and Mitchell were good friends. They went on hunting trips together all over the world. Very expensive hunting trips."

Cody uttered a few well-chosen curses under his breath, though he had no idea whom they were directed toward. Probably himself for letting Sarah play with his emotions. "I'll keep my end of the bargain. We'll leave here first thing in the morning."

He broke the connection before Daniel had a chance to argue further.

Sarah stared at him. "I take it that was Daniel Austin."

"Yeah." The response came out far gruffer than he'd intended.

"Why is it that you get upset every time you talk to him? I've never known him to be anything but nice."

"Exactly how did you meet him?"

"He used to tease me when he came into the office, mostly because I never recognized him. One day he'd come in clean-shaven and debonair, downright handsome for a man in his forties. The next time I'd see him, he'd be twenty pounds overweight with thick glasses and thinning hair."

"That's Daniel. The master of disguises."

"It hit me hard when I heard he was dead. Not that I'm supposed to hear that kind of thing, but I did."

"How did he contact you about copying the files? Did he come to your office?"

"No. He called me on the phone and asked me to meet him in this bar downtown—one of those places Todd would have died if he thought I'd gone into alone."

"And you just rushed out to a sleazy bar to meet a dead man?"

"He obviously wasn't dead if he called me. Besides, I trust Daniel more than anyone else I know. He's been with the department for years. Next to Mitchell Forbes, he's probably the most respected agent around. If he tells you something, you can count on it."

Cody threw up his hands, irritated with himself for taking part in this conversation. "Get some sleep,

Sarah,'' he said, tired of dealing with a situation he couldn't change. "You'll need it before this is over."

"What about you? Where will you sleep?"

"On the floor." He reached across her and retrieved the extra pillow.

She patted the space beside her. "There's room in the bed, and you'd be a lot more comfortable."

"I don't think so, Sarah." He unbuttoned his shirt, slipped it from his arms and tossed it across the foot of the bed. "I found a quilt in one of the chest drawers. I'll make a pallet."

"You prefer the floor to sharing a bed with me?"

"Yeah, strange as that may seem." He liked his snakes in the grass to hiss instead of smile before they bared their fangs.

"You are strange, cowboy." She shook her head, dismissing him as if he were some kind of kook.

Actually, he had that same feeling. It was definitely a first, turning down an invitation to sleep with a sexy woman. A sexy, traitorous, *pregnant* woman. The floor would be just fine.

CODY PULLED the shades on the windows, leaving the room pitch dark, and quiet except for the sound of Sarah's rhythmic breathing. Evidently guilt did not keep her awake nights.

He toed out of his boots and stretched out in the chair, resting his feet on the side of the bed. Slowly his thoughts turned away from Sarah Rand and back toward the Smoking Barrel.

Mitchell Forbes, a real Texas hero. A rotten father who'd let his son and the woman he'd gotten pregnant live through hell while he accumulated land and money and made a name for himself in the annals of Texas lawmen. But Mitchell as a traitor? He just couldn't swallow that.

He reached for the pistol he always kept within reach. Cold, hard, deadly. It was the only thing Cody had left that he could still count on. Finally he fell into a restless sleep.

Hours later, his mind drugged with sleep, he woke to the sound of tapping. Padding across the floor in his stockinged feet, he retrieved the beeper from the chest where he'd lain it. The number was the one for the Smoking Barrel, only this time it was followed by 7-6-7.

His muscles tightened, and a surge of adrenaline set his nerves on edge. Seven, six, seven. SOS. Moving as quietly as he could, he picked up the phone by the bed and called the Smoking Barrel. There was always a chance it wasn't Mitchell Forbes at all. One of his buddies might need him.

Penny Archer answered on the first ring. "I have bad news," she said as soon as she heard his voice. "Real bad news."

"Is it Mitchell?"

"I'm afraid so."

Chapter Four

Cody tried desperately not to feel anything at all at Penny's pronouncement, and failed miserably. "Was there another heart attack?"

"Yes."

Her voice cracked on the word, and he fought to keep his own steady. "He's not..." He couldn't bring himself to say the word.

"No, he's not dead, Cody. At least not yet, but he is back in the hospital." She hesitated, and when she continued, her tone was pleading. "I know that something happened between you and Mitchell, Cody, but whatever it is, let it go. You have to come back to the Smoking Barrel. Now."

"I can't do that."

"You *can*. You just *won't*. You're stubborn, Cody Gannon. Just like Mitchell. It's no wonder the two of you are always butting heads."

"I'm out of Texas Confidential, Penny. I'm working with someone else now, and I have a job to do."

"Whatever you're doing, it can't be as important as being with Mitchell at a time like this."

"I can't believe he wants everyone sitting around the hospital feeling sorry for him."

"He doesn't. He's acting like the heart attack is a minor inconvenience and that no one should miss work because of him. But we're all worried."

"*All* of you? Then how come you're the only one who called?"

"What is it around here that I don't take care of? Besides, it doesn't matter who called. The point is that Mitchell needs you."

"Mitchell Forbes doesn't need me. He never has." The statement stuck in his throat, not because it was harsh, but because it was true. "I'm sorry, Penny." And he was. Sorrier than any of them would ever know.

"Then you won't come?"

"I told you. I can't."

"What will I tell Mitchell when he asks for you?"

"Tell him I'm out of his hair—this time for good. He'll thank you for the news."

"You have to come back sometimes, Cody. What will I do with the Christmas cards you left hanging on your wall?"

"Save them for me."

"I already did. They're in the second drawer of the desk in the parlor."

Penny kept talking, but Cody stopped listening. His mind took over, dragged him into the distant past, into the helpless and defeated state he had lived in back then. Finally, Penny said a bitter goodbye, and he dropped the receiver back into its cradle.

"Is it morning already?"

The voice stabbed into his thoughts and yanked him back to the present. For a second he'd forgotten all about Sarah. Now she was awake and staring at him.

"It's the middle of the night," he said. "Go back to sleep." He bent and retrieved his jeans from the floor, holding on to the bed rail while he wiggled his legs into them and tugged them over his boxer shorts.

"Don't get all modest on my account." Laced with grogginess, Sarah's voice was deep and sexy, at least it sounded that way to Cody. She rubbed her eyes with the heels of her hands. "You cowboys should try sleeping at night. We do it all the time back in D.C., at least most of us do."

"Yeah, well, haven't you seen the ads? Texas is a whole new country."

"Who were you talking to?"

"Nobody."

"You talked a long time for a wrong number. What did you talk about?"

"Nothing."

"Does this particular nothing have a name?"

"Penny Archer, but she's not the nothing. Her message was."

"Who is she—or is that none of my business?"

"She's a secretary at the—at the ranch where I used to work. A good one except when she's butting into things she knows nothing about, the way she was tonight."

Sarah sat up in bed, suddenly far too interested in what was going on. "So what does a secretary do for a cowboy, type up your correspondence with your horse?"

"Very funny. Obviously you're feeling better than you did when you collapsed into that bed a few hours ago."

"Much better. The enchiladas quit spitting fire."

"Dan will be delighted to hear that."

"But not you?"

She moved her legs under the covers, and the sheet

pulled tighter, accentuating the fullness of her breasts. Cody averted his gaze, angry with himself for noticing. He had enough on his mind without adding problems. "Of course, I'm glad you're feeling better. I'm ready to get this whole thing over with."

"The rest helped me, but you're still the same old grouch. And you look like a man who just lost his best friend."

"I did." He ran his palms along the rough denim of his jeans, as if he could wipe away bad memories with the act. "Only he was never really a friend. It just took me a long time to realize that."

SARAH SQUIRMED in the bed, sure Cody was lying about the phone call. Secretary? She just bet. "That was your girlfriend on the telephone, wasn't it?"

"Penny? No way. More like the bossy big sister—if I had a sister." Cody walked to the window and stared out into the darkness, his shoulders slumped.

"I hate it when the guy I'm with turns his back on me," she said.

"The guy you're with?" He rocked back on his heels. "I'm not *with* you, Sarah, at least not in the way you're making it sound. I'm merely driving you to an appointment. I don't date…"

"Pregnant women." She finished his sentence for him.

"That wasn't what I was going to say."

"Then what were you going to say?"

"Nothing. Go back to sleep. I'm sorry I woke you."

She should drop the conversation and ignore him like he wanted her to do, but she needed to talk even if he didn't. "I'm wide awake now, and it's your fault. You owe it to me to visit a while. A little conversation should put me to sleep."

"Just what a guy likes to hear from a woman."

"It's not personal. Conversation with anyone in the middle of the night puts me to sleep. Unless, of course, it's with someone like Brad Pitt. Then I guess I'd stay awake, but I probably wouldn't want to talk."

Sarah clamped her mouth shut. She was doing it again. Talking a mile a minute and saying nothing. A sure sign she was nervous. Todd hated that about her, said that when she was worried, her tongue got tied in the middle and wagged at both ends.

"So, what do you want to talk about?" Cody asked, stepping toward the bed.

"Tomaso Calderone." She took a deep breath, wishing she could take the words back. Discussing Calderone would not put her to sleep. It would tie her in knots. He was the reason she was nervous in the first place, the reason she was here at all. A cold-blooded murderer who would slit her open and yank out her vitals if this mess she was in went bad.

"Have you ever met him?" Cody asked.

"No, and I wouldn't want to. I know what he's done to people who have crossed him. It makes you wonder, doesn't it?"

"Wonder about what?"

"What kind of childhood he must have had to turn him into such a monster."

"I don't think men like Calderone need a reason to be the way they are. They just *are*." He rested his hand on the top of the headboard. "You don't like Calderone, but you like the color of his money. So what does that make you, Sarah Rand?"

"His money is the same color as everyone else's. He

just has more of it. More than he can ever spend. And that doesn't make me anything.''

"Maybe not in your book."

"You're doing it again, Cody. You talk in circles, but no matter how you twist the words, they always sound like an accusation. You know, I don't mind when people who know me don't like me. That's their pre-rogative. But it really ticks me off when someone who doesn't know anything about me makes snap judgments without even giving me a chance.''

Sarah took a deep breath. She had no idea why she was letting this arrogant cowboy get her so upset except that she'd just crossed over the line—crossed from her safe little world into one where men and women and sometimes children were shot down in the streets or dropped into watery graves.

Or had their bodies cut up in little pieces and …

The memories raced through her mind, and she shivered, suddenly cold through and through. She took a deep breath, determined to make the images disappear. Thoughts like that weren't good for the pregnancy.

Cody reached across the bed and tucked the light blanket around her. The act was unexpected, kind when he was usually so hard-edged with her. She turned to meet his gaze. "Why did you do that?"

"You're shivering. If you like, I can turn some heat on though it must be at least seventy-five degrees in here as it is.''

Cody Gannon was a strange man. One minute he was argumentative and condescending. The next he was concerned about her health. Only the chill inside her wouldn't be helped by a roaring furnace on a late summer night. The only thing that would help was if she didn't feel so alone in all of this.

"No heat, Cody, but there's really no use in you sleeping on the floor. There's plenty of room in the bed."

He narrowed his eyes and stared at her as if she had just proposed that he jump from a flying airplane. "I don't know what you're up to, Sarah, but even if I slept with you, even if we made love until sunup and it was the best I ever had, it wouldn't change anything."

"Make love? Is that what you thought I was asking you to do?"

"It sure sounded that way to me."

"Then you don't listen too well, cowboy." She sat up straight, this time holding the sheet so that all he could see was her face. "I was having a bad case of nerves and thought you were feeling down yourself. A little closeness sometimes helps, but I had no intention of—of being intimate with you."

He stared at her, his mouth open, his ego hopefully slammed down a peg or two. "But just for the record," she continued, so angry she couldn't bite back her words. "If I had made love with you, it *would* have been the best you ever had." She pounded her pillow, plumping it, then reached around and flicked off the light. "Too bad you'll *never* get the chance to find out."

CODY BACKED AWAY, his hands at his sides. He didn't understand Sarah Rand at all, not that he'd ever understood women.

Still, he had the sneaking suspicion that she'd told the truth at least once tonight. She was as fiery as hot peppers and making love to her might well have been the best he ever had. Another time, another place, in another situation—when she wasn't in league with the devil, when she wasn't pregnant with another man's child, and he would have crawled into bed beside her without a second thought.

But he didn't sleep with the enemy. Though, heaven help him, the prospect rattled his brain and taunted body parts that should be immune to such a suicidal prospect.

But he had to keep her and the disk safe while he tried to determine if the man who'd sucked him into this plot really was Dan Austin. If he was, he'd turn Sarah over and Austin could have her arrested and sent to prison.

Sarah, pregnant, behind bars. His stomach and chest burned at the thought, as if someone had just lined them with acid. Now he was the one who needed an antacid.

And not for the first time today, he wished that when he'd ridden away from the Smoking Barrel he hadn't stopped until he'd gotten so far away from Texas that Daniel Austin and Mitchell Forbes and even Texas Confidential couldn't touch his life or his mind.

But then how many billions of miles would that have taken?

PENNY ARCHER walked down the wide hallway on the first floor of the ranch house. Moonlight filtered through the oversize window in the front wall of the library, illuminating her path. The floor creaked beneath her feet, the only sound except her own breathing and the baying of a coyote off in the distance.

Twelve years ago, she would have shuddered at the coyote's baying. But then she had been only twenty-two and lost in grief over her mother's death. That's when Mitchell Forbes had stepped in and offered her a job at the Smoking Barrel.

The house, the land, the life. They belonged to

Mitchell Forbes, and he belonged to them. In a way, she did, too. There was nothing she wouldn't do if he asked her to. Nothing. That's why she couldn't understand the way Cody had just turned his back on Mitchell and on his life as a Texas Confidential agent.

Unless… She took a steadying breath, her mind finally hitting on a possibility she could believe. This could be part of a covert operation, one where it was supposed to look like Cody had quit Texas Confidential. That would explain his suddenly getting angry enough to walk off the job without even submitting a formal letter of resignation.

She stopped in front of the bookcases that fronted the secret elevator. She never went down to the communication center without feeling at least a tingle of the overwhelming excitement she'd felt the first time Mitchell had pushed the button and the bookcases had parted, revealing the secret access.

If she'd had her way, he'd have signed her on as one of the agents and let her go out on the same type of undercover assignments he sent Rafe and Cody and the others on. But he was from the old, old school and didn't think a man should put a woman in harm's way. So the only time she got to face danger was in her dreams—and in her fantasies.

Stepping into the elevator, she pushed the down button, then raked her brown hair off her shoulders and twisted it into a knot, securing it with a small comb from her robe pocket. A few seconds later the doors slid open and the glare from bright overhead lights momentarily blinded her.

"What the hell are you doing down here this time of the night?"

She squinted but didn't have to see to know the

owner of that voice. "I could ask you the same thing, Rafe Alvarez."

"I couldn't sleep, and I didn't want to wake Kendra with my tossing and turning so I just came down here to pace and to shuffle paperwork around."

"Same with me. I just keep thinking of Mitchell stuck in that hospital when you know how he hates being confined." She tugged her chenille robe together and looped the belt into a knot at her waist.

Rafe leaned his muscular six-foot-plus frame back in the swivel chair and propped his booted feet on the desk, smiling just a little wickedly. "Was that black silk I glimpsed beneath that robe?"

"If it was, it wasn't for you. You're an old married man now."

"I'm married, not dead."

Good old Rafe, even when she was so far down in the dumps she couldn't climb out with a rope, he could make her smile. Time was, he could also have had her heart beating a little faster and heat burning in her cheeks as well. But she was past that now.

And he was only teasing anyway. He and Kendra were barely back from their honeymoon and so much in love, they glowed when the other walked into a room. Nice that they got to work together as well. Kendra was a computer whiz, and she'd done wonders with the Texas Confidential data system since coming on board.

"Married is same as dead to me," she taunted.

"Then I guess the sexy nightie is all for Neil. That boyfriend of yours is a lucky man."

"Not nearly as lucky as he'd like to be. Actually, I sometimes wonder why I see him at all. We get along, but there's no magic. Not like there is with you and Kendra.''

"There might be, if you wore that sexy nightie for him.''

"No. Magic is either there or it isn't." She crossed the room and perched on the edge of the desk that supported Rafe's feet. She had more serious matters on her mind tonight than her own love life. "What happened to make Cody leave, Rafe?"

Rafe dropped his feet to the floor with a thud and pushed back from the desk. "No one seems to know for certain, unless Mitchell does. If he knows, he isn't talking, but Brady and Jake both think that Cody and Mitchell had words again."

"Do you think he could just be pretending to quit Texas Confidential, that it's part of some scheme the DPS has cooked up?"

"If it is, it's so undercover, I don't know about it."

"And you wouldn't say if you did." She rubbed the stiff muscles in the back of her neck. But she wasn't quite ready to drop the subject. "What reason did Cody give you for leaving?"

"None. You know Cody, he never talks about anything personal. He just rode out to the stable where I was putting out some fresh hay and told me he was leaving for good."

"What did he say when you asked him why he was quitting?"

"I didn't ask. I figured if it was any of my business, he'd tell me."

"So you just let him walk away without even trying to stop him?"

"He's a man. He can think for himself." Rafe ran his hands back and forth across the chair's armrests.

"You know I'd go to the wire eight days out of seven for Mitchell Forbes, but I can see Cody's side of this, too. Mitchell never treated him the way he treats the rest of us. He was always riding him about something. It was as if Mitchell never fully trusted Cody."

Penny exhaled sharply. "You don't think…" She paused, unwilling to speak the thought that had just come barreling into her mind.

"Go ahead and say it, Penny. It's no worse to say a thing than it is to think it, and you're probably not the first person around here to come to that conclusion."

"I know that Kendra found proof that there really is a leak in the DPS. Do you think that Cody could be the person selling classified information to Calderone?"

"Anything's possible."

"Oh, Rafe, I hope that's not the case. I know Cody's had a hard life, but I can't believe he'd side with Calderone no matter what the man paid him. Not against you and Mitchell and the others."

"So, give the man the benefit of the doubt. No one has anything on him. If they did, Cody wouldn't be walking around a free man."

Penny slid off the edge of the desk and paced the room, the new possibilities churning inside her. She stopped next to Mitchell's desk and looked back at Rafe. "I talked to Cody earlier tonight. I told him about the latest heart attack and asked him to come back to the Smoking Barrel to see Mitchell. He refused."

"You talked to Cody?" Rafe narrowed his eyes and the muscles in his face and neck tightened. "Where was he?"

"He didn't say, but the number on the caller ID was a Texas area code."

"Do you have the number?"

Penny reached into the pocket of her robe and fished out the pink slip of paper. She handed it to Rafe. "It wouldn't be too hard to trace the number and see where he is."

"I don't see what good that would do. If he doesn't want to come back, you can't make him. And if Mitchell thinks he's responsible for the leaks, he wouldn't want him around anyway."

"You're right," she said, suddenly tired and ready to climb back into her own bed. "But I always had the feeling that Cody is Mitchell's special project. He rides him, but he also worries about him. I think finding out that Cody was the leak would just about kill him."

Rafe fingered the note and then laid it next to the telephone. "Did Cody say what he was doing or if he was alone?"

"All he said was that he was working and that I could tell Mitchell he was out of his hair for good." She walked toward the door. "I'm going back upstairs to try to get some sleep."

"You go ahead. I want to finish something I started."

"Okay, I'll see you in the morning."

"Right, but don't mention to anyone else what we talked about tonight."

"Do you mean the fact that Cody might be involved with the leaks?"

"Right. That's only speculation."

Penny nodded in agreement and then stepped back inside the elevator. When she looked back at Rafe, he was picking up the telephone receiver with one hand and holding the pink slip of paper she'd given him in the other. Calling Cody, she was sure. Who else would he be calling in the middle of the night?

By the time she made it to her second-floor bedroom, she could barely keep her eyes open. The last thing she remembered was climbing into bed and whispering a prayer that Mitchell would come back to the Smoking Barrel as bossy and as active as ever. She couldn't imagine life on the ranch without him.

CODY STRETCHED and opened his eyes, instantly aware of his surroundings. He never slept soundly when he was on a case, never relaxed enough to drift into the kind of deep, dreamless state that made him lose his edge.

The blackness of night had softened to the grayness of predawn. Sarah stirred. He stood and walked over to the bed. Eyes closed, her hair disheveled and falling into her face, she looked totally innocent—and entirely too feminine. He was so near he could hear her soft breathing and see the movement of her breasts beneath the thin sheet.

The ridiculous urges inside him strengthened, and Cody forced himself to walk away. Stumbling back to the chair, he found his boots and slid his feet into them. He needed to get out of here. Now. Before he forgot who Sarah really was. Before he forgot that he was here to do a job and nothing more.

"NO, NO, YOU CAN'T take my baby away." Sarah reached for the infant, but every time her fingers got close to the baby, the man took another step backward. Her heart pounded against the walls of her chest and her breath came in short painful gasps. So close, her baby was so close, but she couldn't reach her. She opened her mouth to scream for help, but nothing came out.

The man shook his finger at her. "Naughty, naughty, naughty. You were a bad, bad girl, Sarah Rand."

A bad girl. She was, and they were taking her baby.

The baby started to wail, and Sarah lunged for her. Only there was no baby. There was...

Sarah woke with a start. The dream. The same miserable dream she had every night in one version or another. The past, the present, all tangled together and always someone was taking her baby away.

Breathing easier now, she pressed the palms of her hands against her growing belly. Not hard, just enough to feel the roundness, to imagine that her baby could feel her touch. "No one will take you away from me," she whispered. "I'm not a bad girl. I'm a woman and I'm doing something right and good. You'll be proud of me."

Her heart stilled, and she strained to make out forms from the dark gray shadows that filled the room. An empty chair. The pine dresser. The narrow table. But no cowboy.

She muttered a word unfit for a lady and threw her legs over the side of the bed. Cody should be here. She should hear his breathing and see his lean body sleeping in the chair or stretched out on the quilt on the floor. But the room was empty.

Frantically, she tiptoed to the window and stared out into the darkness. The moon was half-hidden behind a low layer of clouds, but still there was enough light to see that the truck was gone.

Turning, she surveyed the room again. She was all alone in a dilapidated hunting cabin miles from an airport, worlds away from D.C. She flicked on the lamp, grabbed her suitcase and rummaged through it until she found the oversize T-shirt and the pair of baggy, elastic-waist jeans.

Fear and anger mingled, lashing and snarling inside her. She had risked her freedom to steal those files, and for what? To be deserted by some arrogant cowboy pretending that his job was to keep her safe. Some bodyguard he'd turned out to be.

Her hands shook as she took off the slip she'd slept in and pulled on the jeans. Her hair fell across her face and into her eyes as she jerked the yellow shirt over her head. She tugged it into place, pushed the hair back from her face, then bent to find her shoes. They sat neatly under the edge of the bed, though she was sure she'd kicked them off last night, too sick to care where they had fallen. Maybe the jerk cowboy did have one virtue. Apparently he was neat. Neat and quiet as he sneaked away in the night.

Swearing under her breath, she headed for the bathroom. She'd at least wash her face and brush her teeth. Then she'd look presentable when she explained to the night watchman that she'd been deserted and needed someone to drive her into San Antonio.

She was halfway there when the sound of gunfire stopped her in her tracks.

Cody. It had to be Cody, but what was he firing at and where had he been? Too stunned to think straight, she raced to the door and yanked it open. The night watchman lay in the dirt not twenty yards from her door, his arms over his head, blood pooling around him. She started toward him, but a brusque male voice stopped her.

"Don't bother. He's dead."

The voice did not belong to Cody.

Chapter Five

The man stepped from the shadows, the gun still clutched in his right hand. Before Sarah had time to react, he'd shoved her back inside the cabin, pulling the door shut behind him. "Unless you want to meet the same fate as that stupid guard, I suggest you stay calm and do what I say."

She tripped over a woven throw rug. Throwing up her hands, she managed to grab the edge of the dresser and steady herself. "Who are you?"

"Your worst nightmare, and if you want to live to see it end, hand over the files you stole from the DPS."

The disk again. She should have known. Her gaze flew to the hanger where Cody had hung her coat last night. The hanger was empty.

The man moved his gun in a threatening circle. "I'm not a patient man."

She stared at him, unable to make her body react or her mouth work. His face was a leathery patchwork of rigid features and thin, drawn lines, his body muscular and intimidating. He meant business, but she didn't have what he demanded.

Apparently Cody had found it while she slept. Now

he was gone and so was the disk. So much for "if you need anything, I'll be here."

"The disk." The man's voice was a low growl. "Hand it over."

"It isn't here."

The man's eyes darkened, and his free hand clenched into a tight fist. "You're lying."

"No." She could feel the sting of his stare on her skin, acidic and dirty. "Look, mister—whoever you are—I'd give you the disk if I had it, but I don't."

"That's real nice of you, Miss Rand. So what do you think I'm going to do now?"

"I think you're going to get out of my room. Why wouldn't you?"

"Guess I'm just not that kind of guy." He played with the threatening pistol, twirling the trigger guard on his index finger before he pointed the gun at her stomach. "I want the files, Sarah, and I want them now. I don't think I can make myself any clearer."

No, she understood exactly what he meant. He expected her to hand over the disk she didn't have. If she didn't, she'd be history. And if she did, she'd probably still be history. Any way you went at it, she ended up dead—unless she could think of some way to distract him long enough to make a break for it.

"Okay, I'll give you the disk," she said, not sure where she was going with this new strategy, but desperation called the shots.

"I thought you might see it my way."

"You're a very convincing man." The lie indicating she could produce the disk had bought her a minute but now she had no idea what to do with it. She glanced around the room, searching for anything that might give her an idea. She turned, banging her toe on the corner of the bedpost. It smarted fiercely and her eyes watered like crazy.

The man stepped closer, his breath hot, the threat in his eyes tearing away what little hope she still held on to. He moved the pistol, this time skimming it along the flesh of her right temple. "You've wasted enough of my time. Hand over the disk. Now."

"I would but…the disk is at the airport."

His brows shot up. "Care to explain what it's doing there?"

Yeah, as soon as she came up with an explanation. "I, ah, I didn't trust the man that met me there. I ran away from him and hid the disk in the parking garage."

"You need to be a little more specific. The parking garage covers a lot of territory."

"I'll show you where it is, but only if you promise to let me walk away once it's in your hands."

"No use to wait for the airport. Just tell me where you hid the diskette and I'll have an accomplice check it out. If he finds it, you live to play another day."

"I'll take my chances in a parking garage," she said, keeping her voice steady. "I like my odds better with people and security guys around."

"Is it the odds you like or do you think your cowboy buddy is going to ride to your rescue again?"

Again. So he did know about her previous attack. "If you think I'm gullible enough to depend on the cowboy, you've been listening to too many dumb blonde jokes."

He stared at the rumpled bedsheets. "I was just thinking about what went on in here last night before Cody Gannon ran out on you."

She exhaled sharply and clenched her hands so tightly her fingernails cut into her palms. Whoever this monster was, he seemed to have a lot of information. "What do you know about Cody Gannon?"

"Enough to know that he can't be trusted. What I don't understand is why he left you here alone." He ran his thumb along the grip of his pistol. "Unless you're lying to me and Gannon already has the disk. Is that it, Sarah? Is he delivering it by himself?"

She swallowed hard, knowing that if he thought Cody had the disk, he'd kill her in the fraction of a second it took to pull the trigger. "Cody left because he's a coward," she said. "He was all nice at first. Then he got scared and said he didn't trust me. He cut out while I slept."

"So Cody just collected a little interest on the amount owed him before he left. Looks like he enjoyed it." The man stared at the bed. "Just you and Cody Gannon. A regular little love nest." Smirking at whatever perverted images played in his mind, he threw back the twisted covers.

Her black coat poked from beneath the blanket. It had been there all along, hidden by the quilt she'd tossed aside when she'd crawled from beneath the covers. Evidently Cody had found the disk she'd hidden so carefully and then tossed the coat across the bed.

She forced herself to make eye contact with the gun-toting monster. Her best bet was still to ride back to San Antonio with him. And even then, she had little chance of escape.

How could she ever have listened to Mr. Austin? How could she have believed that it would be as simple as he said, that one quick act from her could accomplish what countless undercover lawmen throughout the whole state of Texas hadn't been able to do?

"If you want the disk, you'll go with me to the airport,'' she repeated, her voice strangely calm now that her options had been narrowed to one. "If you don't want it, then kill me here."

"A tempting thought," he said, "but it's your show—for now." He put a hand on her shoulder and shoved her toward the door. "Lead the way. My car is just outside. Just remember, I'm only a step behind, and when I shoot, I shoot to kill."

Sarah didn't doubt it for a minute. She started toward the door and then stopped. "I need my coat." When he didn't protest, she went back for it. She felt for the hard plastic rectangle that rested beneath the nylon lining. It was still there, secure in the pocket she'd sewn for it.

So, Cody hadn't found the disk after all. He'd just had enough of her, just like everyone else in her life who'd ever mattered. The thought stung even when she was fighting for her life. With a quick motion, she threw the coat over her shoulders before stepping out of the cabin and into a new world of the unknown.

The blood was the first thing she saw—a crimson river that splattered the dirt and filled the cracks in the broken asphalt. Then her gaze moved to the body, lying facedown, just past a broken flower pot.

Her stomach turned inside out, and she had to force her feet to move past the slain guard. A mosquito buzzed around her face. An owl hooted in the distance. A bug scurried across her path. Strange the simple things you noticed when reality became too macabre to bear.

She stopped at the car door and looked back at the cabin. She hadn't really seen it from the outside last night. She'd been too tired to notice. Then, Cody had taken charge, taking care of her with a tenderness she'd never expected from the cocky cowboy.

There one minute. Gone the next. The story of her life.

"Get in." The man opened the car door and shoved her inside. Her feet had barely cleared the opening when he slammed the door shut and raced around the back of the car. She closed her eyes and waited for him to join her.

The sound of gunfire exploded, and she ducked instinctively, throwing her hands over her stomach. Bullets hit and ricocheted off the back of the car. For a second, she thought the man had changed his mind, decided to kill her here and now, but a second later she heard his wail and saw him fall onto the back of the car. Blood gushed from his right arm, but he rocked off the trunk and managed to reach the door on the other side of the car. Acting on impulse, she threw her weight against the door handle and half fell, half jumped from the seat.

"Get down!"

Someone yelled the obvious, but her coat caught on something inside the car. She yanked it free as the tires of the car skidded in the dirt, then sped away.

She doubled over, clutching her stomach.

"Are you all right?"

"Cody." She looked up to find him rushing toward her. "Where did you come from?"

"The river. The watchman said he'd keep an eye on the cabin while I went to the office for coffee. I took the time to walk down to the river. When I heard the shot, I raced back and that's when I saw you and the man with the gun."

"But your truck was gone."

Cody hunched over her, his breathing still choppy, his muscles tense. "I moved the truck into the bushes as soon as I got you settled last night. I didn't want to take a chance on someone spotting it." He wrapped an arm about her shoulder. "Did he hurt you?"

"No, but he would have if I'd given him that dreaded disk." She turned and looked toward the body that lay by the steps. "We need to call an ambulance."

"It's too late for that. He's dead." Cody continued to stare at her. "Is something wrong with the baby?"

"The baby?" She shook her head, finally realizing that she still had one hand beneath the swell of her stomach. "Nothing hurts." She exhaled slowly, clearing her lungs and trying to think straight. "Mother and child are both fine."

"If this baby makes it, he's going to be one tough *hombre.*"

"He, or *she.*" And Sarah wasn't going to even consider the possibility that the baby might not make it. "I think we should call someone. We can't just leave the watchman lying there in his own blood. He'll have family. Maybe a wife."

"We can't help him, and we can't stay around to answer questions." His voice was low and steady but he seemed years older than the sexy young cowboy who'd met her at the airport less than twenty-four hours ago. "I'm not sure how many people know about the disk, Sarah, but someone's tried twice to kill you for it."

"And the third time is always the charm."

"I don't plan for there to be a third time, at least not on my watch." He helped her to her feet. "But we have a lot to talk about and this isn't the place to do it. I want you to wait inside the cabin while I get the truck.

I'll pick you and your luggage up at the door. The faster we move, the better our chances of getting out of here without being followed.''

She didn't miss the urgency in his voice or the nudge of his hand on the small of her back. She started walking. "Do you think the man will come back?"

"I don't think this is over, if that's what you mean."

"But he's wounded. You hit him in the arm, just below the shoulder. I saw the blood."

"When you agreed to deliver that disk, you jumped into the game with the big boys, Sarah. You don't get a million dollars for simple courier services."

"I didn't *offer*. I was persuaded. And no one mentioned a million dollars."

"That's not the way I heard it."

"Then you heard wrong."

Cody stopped at the door. "In that case, I'd love to hear your side of this. Later."

He turned and walked away and Sarah stepped back inside the cabin, shaking from fear, anger, shock. And probably from a million other emotions she couldn't put a name to just now. But at least she was alive. And Cody Gannon, aggravating or not, was obviously the right man to be with if you had a killer on your trail.

A DOZEN CONCERNS scuffled for control of Cody's mind as he pulled away from the cabin. The one that kept jumping to the forefront was the lady sitting beside him. She'd been through a lot since he'd met her at the airport yesterday. She was feisty, tough, and in spite of everything, she hadn't fallen apart even though he'd almost let her get killed back at the cabin.

He tugged his Stetson low on his forehead as old aggravations knotted and twisted inside him. Two years with Texas Confidential and he couldn't even lose a tail on a back road. He'd worked with some of the best agents, but he'd never been able to walk their walk.

Not that the others had ever expected too much of him. Why should they? They'd been hired for their expertise. He'd never been anything more than a misfit, in trouble more often than he'd been out. His hiring had been strictly Mitchell Forbes's doing. Now he realized it was a feeble attempt at making up for what the old coot hadn't been man enough to do when it might have counted for something.

Sarah squirmed in the seat beside him, curling one leg under her and shrugging out of her coat. "How long will it take us to get to Mexico?" she asked, not bothering to turn in his direction.

"It depends on the route we take and how often we stop. If we stay on the back roads and off the Interstate, it could take most of the day."

"Does that count stopping for food?"

"Food and a few gas and bathroom stops. Are you hungry?"

"I could eat. I was never much of a breakfast eater before. Toast sometimes with my coffee, but nothing else. Now I wake up starving. I'm eating for two, you know?"

"I know. I'll find somewhere to grab a bite." He kept his eyes on the road ahead of him. He handled Sarah better when he wasn't looking at her. "Are you sure food is all you need?"

"No. I need to deliver this disk and get out of Texas. I'd prefer to be somewhere where people don't shoot at me."

"Then you should be more careful who you choose for your playmates."

She focused her gorgeous emerald eyes on him. ''What is it with you, Cody Gannon? One minute, you treat me like I just stepped out of a bucket of green slime. The next, you're risking your life to save mine. I just don't get it.''

He didn't get it himself. He knew what Sarah was. And yet back there at the cabin, when he'd seen the gun pointed at her head while she was being led to the killer's car, he'd experienced emotions he didn't know he was still capable of feeling. They had come over him in a heartbeat, the way they had in that bank two years ago.

In both instances, Cody had experienced such a wave of rage that he could have torn the shooter apart with his bare hands if he'd thought he could do it before the intended victims took a bullet. But today had been different in one way. When it was over, it had taken all the willpower he possessed not to gather Sarah in his arms and hold her close.

The only explanation he could come up with was that the pregnancy changed everything for him. He tried to see Sarah as only another woman contaminated by greed, but when he listened to her talk or looked into her eyes, he only saw a scared, young mother-to-be whose so-called boyfriend had run out on her and on his child.

Not that it was the pregnancy he'd been thinking of last night when the sheet had slipped away and he'd glimpsed the smooth flesh of her breasts peeking out over the silky slip. And it wasn't the pregnancy that had driven him out into the fresh air before dawn. It had been simply knowing he was a man and she was a very desirable woman.

''You didn't answer me, Cody.''

"I don't remember your asking a question."

"Then I'll ask it now. Do you like me at all?"

From the periphery of his vision, he could see her clasp and unclasp her hands. He hated the act. It was part of the innocent and frightened image that was blowing his mind, making him think of her as an innocent victim instead of a cool, calculating enemy who'd bitten off more than she could handle.

Only maybe she was innocent and it was Daniel Austin who was lying. Or maybe the man he'd met in the bar wasn't Austin at all. Or maybe it had just been too long since he'd been with a woman who affected him the way Sarah Rand did.

"I have a job to do, Sarah. Whether I like you or not doesn't really matter."

"I guess it doesn't. But maybe you can explain something while you're at least talking to me."

"Hit me with it."

"Okay. I followed Mr. Austin's instructions to the letter, except for that one incident at the airport when I tried to ditch you. I did what I was supposed to do, so who are these men who are following us and how do they know about me or the disk?"

"I don't know, but I plan to find out, one way or another, and we don't have any time to lose. So what about breakfast? Eggs over easy and truth on toast. And this time I need to know exactly what kind of deal you cut with Dan Austin."

"Then find a diner, and be prepared not to like what I have to tell you."

Chapter Six

Cody watched Sarah gobble down a short stack of pancakes with strawberries and a glass of milk, amazed that her appetite was so hearty in spite of what she had been through this morning. His was suffering miserably.

As far as he knew, the woman back at the cabin hadn't copied down his license plate, but she could still give the police a description of him and Sarah and his truck. Not that his scratched and well-used vehicle was much different from thousands of others on Texas highways this morning.

Still, to be on the safe side, he'd parked in back of the truck stop, huddled among the big rigs and well hidden from view. And they'd taken a back booth. He could see the door, but Sarah's blond head barely poked above the seat.

Sarah shoved the last bite of pancake around on her plate. "Do you think the cops might think we're the ones who killed the night watchman? His body was right outside the cabin we stayed in."

"They'll at least want to interrogate us. If they find us."

"Then we're actually fugitives from justice."

"More like innocent people running from the killer,

at least innocent of murder charges.'' Stealing government secrets was a different story.

Sarah laid her fork across the plate, leaving the last bite of pancake to soak in a pool of melted butter. ''Do you think the man that's after the disk could be one of Calderone's men?''

She said the name Calderone as if it were a dirty word. But this whole mucked up operation was built around the fact that she was stealing files specifically for the man. He smelled a rat. He was no longer sure if he was traveling with it or working for it. ''Exactly what is in the files that you stole from the DPS, Sarah? And don't give me the runaround about Daniel telling you not to talk. I'm the one who's sticking my neck out to save yours.''

''I don't know the content. All Dan gave me was file names.''

''Do you have the names copied down somewhere?''

''No. Mr. Austin insisted we leave no tracks that could be followed.''

''But they were files that you had access to?''

''No. I had to break into them. At first I didn't think I could, but then by accident I discovered Mr. Cochran's password.''

''By accident?''

''I had worked late one night, finishing up some reports he insisted on having immediately. I was about to enter his office to hand them to him when I noticed a series of stars on his screen. You know, the little asterisks that indicate you're typing in a confidential code?''

''So if it was in code, how did you get it?''

''I watched his fingers and picked up the last five symbols in the letter-number sequence. Then all I had to do was wait for the perfect opportunity to slip into his office, log on to his computer and experiment with the symbols until I got the first two right. The first was *B. B* as in baby. It seemed a good omen.''

A good omen for a bad deed. ''Did you run into any difficulty copying the files?''

''No, once I used the password, I could go right to them. No offense, Cody, but the trouble started when I hooked up with you.''

''Yeah, Thrill-a-minute Gannon, that's me.'' His feeble attempt at humor fell flat. He tried to picture Sarah in the scenario she'd just described. Cool, calculating, sneaking into her boss's office and stealing confidential government files. The image didn't gel. He kept seeing a pixieish, pregnant lady who talked a mile a minute when she got nervous. ''Didn't you have any second thoughts about what you were doing?''

''Second, third and a dozen more. I was scared to death. My heart thumped so loudly, I thought the guard on duty would hear the clamor and come barging in to arrest me.''

''But still you went through with it?''

''I have the disk. That's proof enough, isn't it?''

''It's not proof to me. I haven't seen it.''

''I *have* it. That's all you need to know. My deal is with Daniel Austin.''

The waitress stopped at their booth and refilled Cody's coffee cup. She started to pour more for Sarah, but she waved her away.

''Too much caffeine's not good for the baby. I'd like some orange juice, though, if it's not too much trouble.''

''No trouble at all, sweetie. It's my job.'' She added the price of the juice to the ticket and laid the rectangle of paper on the table next to Cody. ''I'll take that when you're ready." She turned and directed her gaze at Sarah's protruding stomach. "When's the baby due?"

"The end of December. She'll be my little tax deduction."

The waitress smiled and then looked back to Cody. "Guess you'll like that, Daddy."

He choked on his coffee, and a few drops spewed from between his locked lips. He grabbed for his napkin and covered his mouth.

"Oops. Guess that word daddy doesn't go down too well yet." She was laughing as she walked away.

Cody wasn't.

Sarah glared at him. "You didn't have to cause a scene over the waitress's mistake. I didn't go all to pieces last night when you registered us as a married couple, though I wasn't a bit more pleased at having someone think I was your wife."

"I'm sorry. I just wasn't expecting it. That's all."

"Yeah, right." She pushed back from the table. "I've changed my mind about the orange juice. I'll tell the waitress to cancel the order. You can finish your coffee and pay the ticket while I go to the ladies' room."

She picked up her purse and coat from the seat beside her.

"Just leave those here. I'll keep an eye on them."

"You don't trust anyone, do you?"

"Not at the moment. And you can come back here when you finish in the ladies' room. We haven't finished our talk."

"We can finish it right now. What do you want to know?"

"What you're getting out of stealing these files. I'm sure you didn't agree to do it for nothing."

She leaned close, her voice low but biting. "Fine, Cody. You're right. I'm not as noble as you. Dan offered to pay me, a bonus for services beyond the call of duty. I think that's how he put it. If that makes me less of a person in your eyes, then so be it."

"A million dollars is a damn nice bonus."

"A million dollars?" Her voice rose and her eyebrows arched. "Are you smoking rope? But I'm not doing it for the money, though I know that's hard for you to believe." She stood and glared down at him, her emerald eyes spitting fire. "Is there anything else you want to know?"

"If you didn't do it for the money, why did you do it?"

"Because Tomaso Calderone has gotten by with murder for far too long." She took a deep breath, but didn't look away. "Mr. Austin said the information in the files I copied would prove once and for all who was leaking important data to him. I helped because it was the right thing to do and, if you don't understand that, I feel sorry for you."

Cody watched as she spun away from him and strode across the floor. Livid. Head high. Seductive. That was the word that had come to mind in the airport yesterday. It still fit, but now he had more adjectives to go with it.

Either Sarah Rand was the coolest, most professional liar he'd ever met or else the man in the bar the other night had fed him enough bull to choke a starving coyote.

Cody finished his coffee, fished a ten and a couple of ones out of his pocket and ironed them with the flat of his index finger before sliding them under the ticket. He was more confused than ever when he got up

from the booth and went to meet Sarah, but he knew
what he had to do, and it wasn't deliver her into the
hands of Dan Austin. Or at least the hands of the man
claiming to be Dan Austin. That possibility loomed
larger with each passing second.

But if he wasn't Dan Austin, he was still damn good
at disguises. He could be anywhere, anytime. The
bearded man at the next table. The tall, busty woman
sitting alone in the booth across the way. The tattooed
man flirting with the waitress. Cody would never know
it until the dirty rat pulled a gun and either abducted
Sarah or killed them both on the spot.

His only choice was to take Sarah Rand and go into
hiding until he knew exactly what was going on and
who could be trusted. Somewhere no one would find
them. Somewhere remote. Isolated. Godforsaken. He
knew just the spot.

He and Sarah, all alone and on the run. Sarah and
her dancing eyes. Her turned-up nose. Her sexy smile.
Her way of talking so fast that his mind grew dizzy
trying to keep up. Sarah with the full, pouty lips.

Sarah with another man's child growing inside her.

It was a good thing he'd learned long ago that life
wasn't fair, and only the tough survived. In the next
few days, he'd see just how tough he really was, on the
inside as well as the outside.

SARAH STARED OUT the truck window. A few scrubby
mesquite trees, a lot of cactus, sparse tufts of grass, sage
and a whopping helping of monotony. She stretched
and turned to stare at the man beside her.

Two days ago he would have fit in her fantasy just
fine. A handsome, rugged cowboy. Sexy, smart and
brave. Even tender at times, though those times were

short-lived. A guy like that could fit in anybody's fantasy, could have been pictured on her tote bag along with the saying.

But that was only the surface Cody Gannon. What apparently lay beneath the surface was a lot less inviting. He brooded, accused, choked on the word daddy.

A jackrabbit hopped from a clump of yellowing brush at the side of the road. She followed the movements of the kangaroo-like creature until it disappeared from sight. "Is this the scenic route?"

"About as scenic as it gets in West Texas. But we will see some mountainous regions later."

"West Texas as in *not* on the way to Mexico?"

"You got it."

"Don't knock yourself out with those detailed explanations." He didn't bother with a comeback. She stretched her legs and turned to face him. "Where are you taking me?"

"Hopefully somewhere your would-be assassin doesn't follow us. A hunting cabin in the Davis mountains."

"Does it belong to you?"

"No."

"How will we get in?"

"If it's locked, there's always a key taped to the bottom of the rocker on the front porch. But don't worry. It will be deserted this time of the year, especially with the owner in the hospital recovering from a heart attack."

There it was again, that unexpected strain to Cody's voice. The same as it had been the other night when he'd talked to the woman named Penny on the phone. She felt certain he hadn't given her the full story about that. Still, he was overstepping his bounds.

"Don't you think you should have asked me before you decided to change our plans?"

"Okay, Miss Rand, do you want to dance into the killer's hands without a fight or would you prefer a chance at staying alive?"

"Since when did Daniel Austin become the enemy?"

"Since I've had time to think more about what happened this morning. I was exceedingly careful last night, and I'm almost a hundred percent convinced that no one followed us to that fishing camp. That means that the man who showed up to kill you and steal the disk this morning had to find out where we were some other way. My guess is it was from one of the two phone calls I made from the cabin."

Two calls, but only one had been to Daniel Austin. "Could your ex-secretary have something to do with it? That Penny woman."

"Very unlikely, but I'm not ruling out the possibility that someone from the ranch could."

"I don't understand. Why would someone at a ranch in west Texas be interested in DPS files?"

"I was hoping I wouldn't have to tell you this, but I don't see any way around it."

"Tell me what?"

"There's a group of highly specialized cowboy lawmen in Texas who work undercover and whose sole purpose is to stop Tomaso Calderone."

"Texas Confidential?"

His brows knitted over his piercing blue eyes. "Evidently not as secret as they think if even the office staff at the DPS know about us."

"I'm not *just* an office worker. Not just a secretary, either. I'm an administrative assistant with security clearance to handle confidential material, though I don't actually see any of the highly classified documents or correspondence. None of the clerical staff does.''

''But you obviously know about the operations of Texas Confidential.''

''I am aware that the agency exists and that it is run by Mitchell Forbes. That's pretty much the extent of my knowledge. I have no idea who the agents are or what types of assignments they go out on.'' She stared at him. ''The question is how do you know about them?''

''Because I'm one of the agents. At least I was until a week ago.''

She gulped. No wonder Cody didn't seem like your ordinary cowboy. He wasn't one. He was part of the legend. Her insides coiled and uncoiled in rapid succession. She'd wanted excitement, but she'd never dreamed she'd actually be racing around the back roads of Texas with a Texas Confidential agent.

No, make that an ex-Confidential agent. ''Why did you resign? There are agents for the DPS who'd shoot themselves in the foot to get a chance to work with Mitchell Forbes.''

''To each his own.''

He wasn't getting off that easily. ''I've answered all your questions. You owe me the same. Why did you leave?''

''It's a long story.''

''Look, I know you don't like conversations that last over a minute or two, but we can do this in segments. A few long sentences between every jackrabbit sighting.''

''Drop it, Sarah. I'm out of the loop. It's not important why.''

His voice was gruff, but she recognized the strain for

what it was this time. Pain. Regret. Funny, she never thought of men having vulnerabilities, never would have thought that someone as tough as Cody Gannon would hurt. Obviously she was wrong.

She weighed his words about the phone calls. "It must have been someone at the ranch, Cody. Daniel Austin had no reason to send someone to kill me for the disk. All he had to do was wait. I was bringing it to him."

"Maybe he lacks patience. Or maybe he'd never intended on meeting with you at all. Right now I have serious doubts that the man we're dealing with is the *real* Dan Austin. If he is, I doubt his allegiance is still with the DPS. I do know that the story he gave me is far different than the one you told back at the truck stop."

Sarah listened as Cody described his bizarre meeting with the pretend drunk in the bar. Listened and shivered as her blood grew cold. If the man she'd trusted hadn't told her the truth, she could be…stealing files for Tomaso Calderone.

Images clouded her mind. The plain, brown box arriving at the office. Her eager fingers as she'd torn into it. And then the bloody pieces of…

"Do you know what Calderone does to people who double-cross him, Cody? He cuts them up into little pieces and mails them home. I opened one of those boxes my first week on the job at the DPS. An agent who'd tried to infiltrate Calderone's ranks."

CODY HEARD the horror in Sarah's voice even before he turned and saw the paleness of her face, felt the shaking spasms of her body. He slowed and pulled to the narrow shoulder of the road. In seconds he'd cleared the space between them and wrapped his right arm about her shoulder, pulling her into the shelter of his arms. "It's okay, Sarah. You'll be safe. I won't let anyone hurt you."

"You can't protect me against Calderone. No one can."

Her eyes filled with tears, and Cody shuddered at his own emotions. He was holding and trying to comfort a woman he had no logical reason to trust, yet he was overwhelmed with a feeling of protectiveness he couldn't explain. One he'd never felt before. Or maybe he had. Years ago.

He'd failed then. He'd been no match for Frank Gannon's fists when they'd plowed into his mother. But he wasn't a boy anymore, and he wouldn't fail now. "We'll work through this, Sarah. I'm not sure how right now, but we will."

"We have to go to the DPS, Cody. We have to tell them what I've done."

"I don't think that's a good idea."

"We don't have a choice."

"We need to find out what's going on, Sarah. Someone is setting you up. If you go to the DPS now you'll be arrested for stealing government files."

"No. I can't be. If I go to jail, there'll be no one to take care of my baby." Her back stiffened. "I'll do anything to have my child born healthy and safe and for her to know how much I love her. I won't let Calderone or the DPS take that away from me."

"Then we better get moving." He reached over and opened the glove compartment and dug around until he found a couple of unused napkins from his last stop at a fast-food chain. He pressed them into her hand.

''Wipe your eyes and blow your nose. We have work to do.''

She did. He scooted across the seat and settled in behind the wheel. ''From here on out, we have to act on the assumption that Calderone is behind the attempts on your life, that he was behind your stealing the files.''

''But we don't even know for certain that the man we talked to was a fake.''

''At this point, the evidence points in that direction. And, unless I miss my guess, someone at the DPS helped set you up.''

''Then like it or not, we're a team, Cody Gannon. Lined up square against a national enemy. A lot like the hero and heroine in a James Bond movie.''

''Look around you.'' He nodded toward the passing scenery. ''Forget James Bond. This is John Wayne, all the way.''

And like the Duke at the Alamo, all the odds were stacked against them. No need to mention that to Sarah just yet. She was smart. She'd figure it out soon enough for herself, if she hadn't already.

''THIS IS NOT what I expected.''

Cody set the bag of groceries he was carrying on the counter then walked to the entrance of the den to find out what had intrigued Sarah.

She performed a semipirouette, surveying the room and talking with her hands. ''I'll give you that this place is rustic. The timber's rough-hewn and the floor doesn't look finished, but that fireplace looks like something right out of *Architectural Digest*. It's mammoth, and the stones give it such character. And there's even a plush leather couch in here.'' She bounced on the cushion. ''I've *lived* in places not nearly this nice.''

"So have I, but this is still just a hunting cabin."

"You didn't say who it belonged to."

"Mitchell Forbes. Who else?"

"Wow. I like his taste." She strolled about the huge den, eyeing each animal head that looked over the room. "Did he kill all of these magnificent animals around here?"

"No, some of the larger game were bagged in Montana and Alaska. Actually, Mitchell doesn't hunt much anymore. He's too occupied with stopping Calderone. But he still comes up here occasionally and he lets the rest of us use the cabin when we get a hankering to hunt something that doesn't fight back with machine guns."

Cody walked back to the kitchen to finish putting away the groceries. Sarah followed. "Is Mitchell Forbes really as impressive as his reputation paints him?"

"Mitchell's tough. Determined. A man's man."

"But you don't like him?"

"I never said that."

"You didn't have to. Your expression and voice did."

"Maybe I just know him better than most. But it doesn't really matter what I think about him. Least of all to him."

"See, bitterness drips from your voice when you talk about him, and you get this gray aura all around you."

"A gray aura, huh? It's just the light in here. The color's brown, not gray. And it's Texas dust, not an aura."

"Go ahead. Make fun of me. But if you stay around me long enough, you'll find out that I can read people the way some people read a book." She reached into one of the grocery bags and pulled out a couple of cans of tomatoes. "Shall I put these in the pantry?"

"One of them. You can leave the other on the counter. I'll use it in tonight's stew."

"You can cook?"

"Simple things. Enough to keep from starving."

"Good, I'm famished, but so tired I think I'd settle for bread and water before I tackled the preparations for a nourishing meal. Ever since I got pregnant, my body seems to crave a lot more rest."

"As long as that's all you crave. We didn't buy any pickles or ice cream and it's a long way back to a grocery store, especially one far enough away from this area that no one would recognize me."

"I can make it fine without pickles or ice cream." Her voice faded to a dusky blur. "Just promise you'll throw in a night without deadly visitors."

Cody grimaced as the now familiar tug twisted around his heart and then settled into a dull pain in his chest. Sarah was looking up at him, her eyes wide and moist, her lips full and pink. A woman who'd earned her merit badge for courage today and yet she looked so vulnerable, it was all he could do not to take her in his arms and rock her to his body.

But he couldn't. Wouldn't. Not with his attraction for her growing stronger with every second he stared into her eyes. He buried his hands in his back pockets and rocked back on his heels. "I'm going out to the truck and get the rest of the supplies. Why don't you grab a shower and rest until dinner's ready? After that we need to decide how we're going to find out what's on that disk. I'd like to…"

He stopped in midsentence, interrupted by the vibration of the pager at his waist. He checked the lighted display for the readout.

Sarah stepped closer. "Is it Daniel, or at least the man who claims to be him?"

"Probably, though it's not the same number as before."

"Maybe you should call the number, just to see what he has to say."

He shook his head. "There's no phone out here. Even if there was, I can't risk giving our location away. Most likely, an isolated place like this would show up as 'out of area' on a caller ID, but I can't be sure. And who knows what kind of tracing mechanism the caller has at his disposal? Crime pays well when you're in the drug business."

"What if it's someone else? What if it's the DPS trying to locate you? What if they found out it was us at the cabin where the man was killed this morning? They may be sending someone to help us."

"That's way too many ifs for my liking. We're on our own, Sarah. You may as well face it." He expected the signs of fear and helplessness to overtake her again, but she held steady.

"In that case, I'm going to take a shower. I'd invite you to join me, but I don't want that brown aura you carry dripping onto my clean body."

She was joking, he knew, but his body reacted anyway. The thought of standing naked under a warm spray with Sarah Rand was too much of a turn-on for him to let it linger in his mind. He turned and walked outside to get the rest of the groceries, hoping the sting of the cool north wind would slap him soundly in the face and kill the wanton urges his libido and Sarah's comment had raised.

CODY SHOVED some wadded up newspaper and a handful of kindling under the logs that were ready and waiting on the cast-iron grate. It was early in the season for a fire, even in the mountains, but the wind was whistling through the cracks around the windows and under the doors.

The ranch house at the Smoking Barrel was tight as a drum, but neither Mitchell nor the other hunters had ever objected to a few drafts at the hunting cabin. He didn't mind them tonight, but Sarah would probably appreciate the fire. She'd been impressed enough with the fireplace.

He struck a match on the sole of his boot and tossed it into the papers. Flames caught and spread, throwing a quick burst of heat in his face. He backed away and dropped to the couch. The place felt cozy, almost homey, with the odors from the simmering stew filling the air. Cody would have to watch the effects, make sure he didn't fall into the traitorous sense of security.

He wasn't sure exactly what he was up against, but if it was Calderone, he and Sarah could run to the ends of the earth and still not dare a carefree breath. Not that he planned to run forever. He'd never run from trouble before, so why start now?

Of course, he'd never had a pregnant accomplice to protect before either. "Accomplice." He said the word out loud. It sounded strange on his tongue.

This morning he'd been sure Sarah was the devil's dance partner, but tonight he was inclined to believe her version of how she'd come to steal the files. But he'd reserve final judgment until he'd actually seen the disk she was supposed to be delivering to a man who called himself Dan Austin. Not only seen it but checked out the type of information it contained.

"Cody."

Her voice startled him. He looked up and saw her standing in the doorway. Her face was pink, scrubbed clean, her hair shiny and wet and clinging to her cheeks and forehead. Her only covering was a towel wrapped sarong style around her body.

He stared, mesmerized, while his will turned to mush and his body grew rock hard.

"Can you help me?" She held up a bottle of green mouthwash. "I can't get the top loose."

"I'll get it." His voice was husky, and if Sarah was half as good at reading people as she said, she had to know what he was feeling right now. He stood and walked toward her, sure that if she didn't stop him, he was going to kiss her.

And unless he was seriously misreading the look in her eyes, she was not going to stop him.

Chapter Seven

The plastic bottle of mouthwash slipped from Sarah's hands as Cody crossed the room. A second later, his lips touched hers. All the emotions of the day poured into the kiss. She forgot the fears, the doubts, the disk, as every cowboy fantasy she'd ever had came to life and then dimmed in the light of reality.

She was trembling by the time he pulled away and struggling for breath. So shaken she could barely think, she leaned against the doorframe. She took a deep breath and forced her body to stand straight and tall. "What brought that on?"

He shrugged his shoulders and stared at the toes of his boots. "I don't know."

"That's a cop-out."

He stepped close again and placed a hand on the wall just above her ear. "Does there have to be a reason for a man to kiss a desirable woman?"

The nearness affected her far too much. She ducked under his arm and stepped away. "There's a reason for everything. You might just be fulfilling a preconceived notion about a man stranded in an isolated cabin with a woman."

"I might, if I had any idea what you're talking about."

"I mean the kiss might just be a macho, obligatory action, so that I wouldn't be disappointed or think you less a man for not trying."

He stared at her as if she'd just landed from Mars. "Did that feel like a macho, obligatory kiss to you?"

She swallowed. "No. It was—nice."

"Nice?" His eyebrows arched and his mouth twisted into a scowl. "You thought the kiss was *nice?"*

"Well, then, *very* nice." Still the understatement of the year, but she wasn't about to admit that on a scale of one to ten, it had been a twelve. Not until she knew what was really going on with him.

He tucked a thumb under her chin and nudged it upward so that she couldn't avoid meeting his gaze. "I don't know why I kissed you, Sarah Rand, except that I'd been wanting to ever since you stepped off the airplane with that silly little tote bag over your shoulder." He leaned in closer. "But I do know this. It had nothing to do with any macho expectations for a man alone with an attractive woman."

"Okay." She needed him to step away from her. Needed the space to breathe and enough distance between them so that he couldn't hear the pounding of her heart. "That clarifies it for me. End of discussion."

"Not quite. I'd like to go on record as saying that you're an unconvincing liar."

"What do you mean?"

"I've had my share of *very* nice kisses in my life. That was not one of them."

"No?"

"No. I'd call it more of a breath stealin', hat tossin', boot kickin' kind of a kiss." He trailed one finger down her right cheek and across her bottom lip before he bent to pick up the mouthwash. He loosened the top and handed it back to her. Her chest felt tight, her insides liquid.

She was overreacting to the kiss, feeling way too much, thinking far too little. She and Cody had been thrown together in a bizarre situation, rife with tension, thick with intrigue and danger.

It wasn't uncommon for two people to bond when they were on the run together. She'd even heard of women in jeopardy falling for their kidnappers, a result of adrenaline overload and hormone misplacement.

Actually she hadn't heard it called that, but her version did sound extremely scientific. So now that she had a handle on what was happening, she just had to remember not to mistake situational attraction for genuine affection. Lust did not equate with love.

Not that she was an authority on what constituted love, she decided as she walked back to the bathroom. She'd certainly been off base with Todd. He'd run at the first sign of complications, and her life had been far less stressful without him. At least it had been less stressful until she'd been taken in by the mock Dan Austin.

She brushed her teeth and rinsed with the stinging antiseptic mouthwash before padding down the wood-planked hallway to the bedroom where Cody had carried her suitcase. Her clothing choices were limited and not exactly suited for a rustic hunting cabin in the Davis Mountains.

Unzipping her suitcase, she shuffled through the offerings, finally deciding on the pair of maternity slacks she'd purchased just before leaving Washington. She had a lot of growing to do to fill them out, but they were comfortable. She wiggled into them, then tugged a loose, mint green cotton sweater over her head, pasting her damp hair to her neck and forehead.

Still barefoot, she posed in front of the mirror. Her figure changed every day, her belly stretching into new shapes, her breasts growing fuller than they'd ever been before. It was the look Todd had warned her about, said she'd hate seeing herself fat and misshapen, be sick about losing her taut stomach and shapely figure.

She ran her hands along the curve of her stomach, pulling the soft fabric of the sweater tight across her paunch. Todd was wrong. She loved the new look. It meant her baby was growing inside her, making a cozy little incubator for herself until she was ready to spring into the outside world.

Sarah wasn't less of a woman. If anything, she was more of a woman. Desirable enough that a man like Cody Gannon had not been able to overcome the urge to kiss her. She touched her fingers to her lips, and her pulse raced as the memory of the kiss filled her mind.

Her stomach moved, like a tickle, or a tiny kick. Too gentle to be sure if it was anything or not, and yet she believed it was her baby telling her that she approved of the rugged cowboy.

Hugging her stomach, she smiled into the mirror. *I will be the perfect mother, my little one. You'll see. I will always be there for you. Always.*

Unless… No. She shook the doubts away. She'd done what she believed to be the right thing and she hadn't been the only one fooled by the man who'd claimed to need her help to stop Tomaso Calderone. Even Cody Gannon had bought into his story for a while, and he was an ex-Texas Confidential agent. And only the smartest and best were signed on by Mitchell Forbes.

Cody Gannon to the rescue. Eat your heart out, you starlets in league with James Bond. This lady would take the cowboy every time.

PENNY ARCHER stood at the foot of her boss's hospital bed. The man was impossible. He was supposed to be recovering, getting strong enough for the quadruple by-pass surgery that was needed to save his life. Instead he was threatening her, trying to coerce her into going out and collecting the details on the night watchman who had been shot at some fishing camp this morning.

"There's no reason to connect that death with any-thing Texas Confidential is involved with, Mitchell. And even if there was, you have been officially relieved of duty until you're out of the hospital and on the mend. We can run things without you, though I know you don't want us to find that out."

Mitchell kicked at the covers that entangled his feet and then scooted up a little higher in the bed. "Did you see the artist's rendition of the man and woman who are suspected in the murder?"

"I saw it." And the same thought that had run through her mind must have occurred to Mitchell as well. She had to find some way to convince him that the man wasn't Cody. "The man and woman had reg-istered as Mr. and Mrs. Carpenter," she said, feigning a mood of nonchalance. "Tourists. And the news re-porter said they're only wanted for questioning."

"They ran from the scene. No matter what the re-porter said, they're suspects."

"But not necessarily guilty. They may have seen the shooting, become frightened and run away. That's what

I would have done if I'd found a body outside my door.''

Mitchell glared at her from beneath his bushy brows. ''You, Penny Archer? No way. You'd have gone after the killer, or killers, single-handedly. It's all I can do to keep you at your computer instead of out chasing criminals as it is.''

''I could do it, you know. Rafe has been teaching me to shoot, and I'm getting very good at it.''

''Don't go getting any ideas, Penny. Your learning to shoot is a precautionary measure, just in case you run into a snake or a rabid coyote while you're out on your horse or if you happen upon trouble when there are no menfolk around.''

''Or if I run into rustlers?''

Mitchell rubbed the stubby growth of hair on his chin. ''Rafe said they struck again yesterday, cut out some of the new calves that haven't been branded. I want you to be careful. Don't go riding too far from the house until we catch them. Who knows what they might try if they're brazen enough to rustle cattle in broad daylight.''

''I can handle them. And, for the record, there are plenty of highly effective women in law enforcement, especially in the field of covert operations.''

''You're exactly right.'' He pulled at his left earlobe and squirmed in the bed. ''If it wasn't for the fact that you're the only one who can find what I need in that office of mine, I'd sign you on as an agent in a minute. See if you're as good at shooting a gun as you are at shooting off that sassy mouth.''

Even in the hospital and facing serious surgery, Mitchell Forbes held on to the gruff exterior that was the signature of his illustrious reputation. Only Penny didn't buy it. The old man had a soft side. She'd glimpsed it often enough when she needed a strong shoulder to lean on or when one of his "boys," as he called his agents, were in danger. Especially Cody.

That's why she wasn't about to tell him that Cody had called the Smoking Barrel last night and that the area code he had called from placed him in the same area as the shooting. She was anxious to ask Rafe if he'd talked to him, but he was out on assignment and had been away from the ranch since before she woke that morning. But she was not eager to continue this conversation with Mitchell.

"I wish I could stay longer," she said, trying to think of some legitimate-sounding reason why she couldn't.

"I want the police report on that shooting, Penny. Have it faxed to the ranch. When you get it, bring it to me."

"We have no reason to meddle in that shooting, Mitchell Forbes, and you know it."

"Don't play games with me, Penny. Anyone with at least one good eye would agree that the drawing looked a helluva lot like Cody."

"Cody is no longer your agent."

His face twisted into a scowl. "He's a Confidential agent until *I* say he's not, and I haven't even seen a letter of resignation, much less signed off on one."

"The man they're looking for was with a woman— a pregnant woman. Cody seldom even dates, and as afraid as he is of commitment, I can't imagine that he's going to be a father."

"Just get me the information. I'd get it myself, but they took the phone out of my room and every time I get up to go searching for one, some nurse grabs me and leads me back to the room. A bunch of snooping pill pushers. That's what they have around here. Between the nurses and Maddie Wells, I hardly get to cover my own nose when I sneeze.''

Penny smiled in spite of herself. Mitchell would never change, and even in the midst of all the trouble, she found that a little comforting. "Neither the nurses nor Maddie would have to stay on your case if you'd follow the doctor's orders on your own. They told you *no stress.* You should listen to them."

He turned to the bedside table and located his silver lighter, reaching around a water glass to retrieve it.

"Mitchell Forbes, you are surely not smoking cigars in the hospital!"

"No. If I did, they'd probably send a nurse in to inhale for me. I just need the feel of something familiar." He worried the lighter, turning it between his weathered fingers. "If you want to ease my stress, get me that report. If you don't, I'll find some way to do it myself."

She exhaled sharply, knowing Mitchell well enough to be certain he wasn't bluffing. "I'll see what I can do."

"And if Cody calls the Smoking Barrel, tell him to get his butt up here. Pronto. I can't imagine what got into him anyway, stamping off the job like he did."

She nodded in agreement. "If I hear from him, I'll give him your message." If Cody called she'd also give him a piece of her mind. And if she could get her hands around his neck right now, she'd strangle him. But she wouldn't pass on the message Cody had left for Mitchell. The man had enough problems without her adding to the pile.

She suspected Cody had his share, too, but she couldn't imagine what they were or why he was so bitter toward Mitchell all of a sudden. Still, she'd do what she could to make sure Cody was at this hospital before Mitchell went into surgery.

If Mitchell died without… No. She couldn't think about that. Mitchell would pull through. And Cody had just better be here.

SARAH SAT at the end of the long pine table, her stomach full, her body more relaxed than it had been in days. "Your stew was delicious. Did your mom teach you to cook like that?"

"Among other things."

"Where is she now?"

"She died."

"I'm sorry."

"So am I, but it was a long time ago. You don't need to feel bad for asking."

"What about your dad?"

The change in Cody was swift and deep. She sensed it before she saw it, but it was visible. Tightened muscles, drawn lips, a hardness that seemed to consume him.

"I'm sorry, Cody. It was just a friendly question. I'm not trying to dive into your past."

"Good. You wouldn't like the water. But Frank Gannon's dead as well. Drank himself to death just before my eighteenth birthday."

"What did you do then?"

"Odd jobs on ranches. Practiced for the rodeo and participated when I could scrape together enough money to pay the entry fees. I had just hit the circuit full time when Mitchell Forbes recruited me."

She turned on the faucet and let the water run until it was hot before adjusting the stopper and squeezing some liquid detergent into the sink. The suds billowed, and she buried her hands beneath the frothy bubbles. "A rodeo cowboy and a Texas Confidential agent. My friends in Washington will be impressed."

"Your friends must impress easily."

"I wouldn't say that. Half of them work for government officials. Of course there's a big difference between some airbag Congressman who thinks he's hot stuff and a real cowboy."

"I'm glad to hear that." He yanked open a drawer and retrieved a clean dishtowel. "Where do your friends think you are now?" he asked, shaking out the towel.

"Gone to Bermuda on vacation."

"By yourself?"

She ran a soapy cloth across one of their stew bowls and then rinsed it under the spray. When she finished, Cody took it from her slippery hands and began wiping it with the dry towel. "I told them I needed some time to get over Todd."

"A man who doesn't want his own child. I can see how he'd be really hard to get over."

"He had a few good points. I can't remember most of them at the moment, but if he was around, he'd be reminding me of them. Actually, Todd was only one of my bad choices. Stealing the files from Mr. Cochran's office was one of my biggest mistakes. I was a fool to think I could make a difference. Now it's my baby who'll pay. A father who doesn't want her and a mother who wants her more than life itself, but the way things look now, won't be with her. I'll either be dead or behind bars."

Cody reached over and brushed away a shock of hair that had fallen across her brow and into her eyes.

"We're not giving up yet. If we can find out who's really behind all of this and get proof that they set you up, you'll have a much better chance of getting off."

She took her hands from the water and wiped them on the towel. "No one has seen the files that I stole, Cody. If I just destroy the disk, maybe no one will ever realize that I copied them. I could go back to my job and pretend that I really was on a vacation."

Cody took her hands in his. "I know you're looking for a way out. I don't blame you, but you've almost been killed twice for that disk. I don't see the man who's after it settling for you just changing your mind."

"So what do I do? I can't run forever. I can't give birth in some isolated cabin in the middle of nowhere."

"I have an idea on the subject."

She pulled her hands from his. She could all but see the wheels turning in his head, and the intensity of his stare set her on edge. "I'm not going to give the files to Calderone, Cody. So, if that's your solution to this, you can forget it. Whatever problem you had with Texas Confidential, it doesn't stretch to include me."

His jaw clenched. "My problem isn't with Texas Confidential. It's with Mitchell Forbes, and it's personal. I wouldn't turn over so much as an unbutchered hog to Calderone."

"Then what is your suggestion?"

"I want to pull the stolen files up on a computer. If I can see what's on the files, I'll have a better idea whether or not it really is Calderone who's looking for them."

"And if it's not Calderone, then it might be the real Dan Austin who contacted us and is waiting for us to deliver them."

"If he is the real Dan Austin and he's telling the truth, that would mean you are lying."

"I'm not lying. So, I guess I have no choice but to go with your plan. The file is here, but we don't have a computer."

"I can't risk calling on anyone I know to borrow one, and if we take the truck back on the highway, the risk is even greater that someone will recognize it or us. Our descriptions have probably been released to police across the state. And the man who wants you dead is still out there looking for you."

A tremor of fear attacked again, creeping up her spine in slow, frigid motion. "How can you be sure no one will find us here?"

"I'm not sure, but I reduced the odds as much as possible. I zigzagged around enough that it's doubtful anyone followed us here. The cabin is so isolated that few people even know it exists."

"The other agents know."

"But I'm banking on the fact that they'll think Mitchell Forbes's cabin is the last place I'd go to hide."

"I've heard that Mitchell Forbes handpicks every man he signs on, that he chooses only the best of the best, the Top Guns in law enforcement."

"For the most part."

"What was your specialty? What made him pick you?"

Cody walked to the window and stared out over the rocky, almost barren landscape. "I had no specialty. No expertise in anything except riding bucking broncs and roping steers."

"I know better than that. I've seen you shoot."

"If I have any claim to fame, I guess that's it. That

and the fact that I don't have any better sense than to jump into a fight when all the odds are against me.''

''But there must be some reason Mitchell Forbes chose you.''

''He had his reasons, all right. He has reasons for everything he does.'' Cody buried his hands in his back pockets. ''I was depositing my rodeo winnings in a bank just outside of Fort Worth, minding my own business. These two thugs walked in and pulled their guns. A bank guard made a foolish move, and one of the robbers grabbed this little girl and started backing out of the bank, holding her in front of him.''

''A little girl about to be abducted by a killer. Every mother's nightmare.''

''This mother started crying and begging the man to let her daughter go. The girl was crying, too. Helpless. Totally vulnerable, and the thug didn't care at all. I went crazy for a second, wanted to tear the man apart with my bare hands, but fortunately I got a grip and assessed the situation. The thugs were panicky and young, and I knew I could take them.''

''But there were two of them with guns.''

''And one half-crazed cowboy who'd witnessed far too much violence against helpless victims in his life. I shot the gun from the hand of one as I dived into the other. I managed to disarm him without shooting him, and the little girl wasn't even harmed.''

Sarah walked up behind Cody and laid her hands on his shoulders, massaging the tight muscles. ''You saved the girl's life.''

''That's what the papers and the TV newsmen said. They made a big thing of it.''

''It was a big thing.''

''It was instinct more than anything else, but Mitchell

offered me a job with Texas Confidential. That was two years ago.''

"The mother must love you."

"She was thankful. So was the daughter. Lauralee Miller. She was only nine at the time. She sends me a Christmas card every year with a picture of herself."

"Do you keep them?"

"I did. Hung them on my bedroom wall at the Smoking Barrel. Lauralee Miller and my mom before she died. I guess those are the only pictures I ever kept."

"Can I see them?"

"You could, but I took off so fast the other night, I forgot to take them off the wall. I'll call one day, if I ever get a permanent address, and have Penny send them to me."

"Hero Cody Gannon. I'm glad you're the man who met me at the airport."

"Me, too." He turned and took her in his arms. "But don't get the idea that I'm some kind of superhero. I'm still just working on instinct."

"That's good enough for me. Just tell me what we have to do."

"All you have to do is stay here and take care of yourself. I'll wait until the wee hours of the morning and break into the Smoking Barrel and log on to the DPS network."

"Add breaking and entering to our list of offenses."

"Not exactly. I still have a key."

"A technicality, but I'll go with you."

"Not this time. I know my way around so well I can move in pitch darkness. You'd slow me down, make it more likely someone would hear or see us."

He planned to leave her here in the cabin. All alone. The way she'd been this morning when the brute had broken in and dragged her to his car. She lifted her face and met his gaze. "Please take me with you, Cody. I'll be quiet. I won't say a word if you tell me not to. Just don't leave me here by myself."

"You'll have to do exactly as I say."

"I will. I promise. I'm getting used to a life of crime."

He touched a finger to her lips. "We're not the bad guys, Sarah. Don't get us confused. The bad guy is the one who pulled that trigger this morning and blew an innocent watchman into eternity. The bad guys are the ones who put illegal drugs into the hands of teenagers and make addicts of them. The ones who destroy anyone and anything that gets in their way of making cold, hard cash."

Old memories crept through her mind. In living color. Blood red. "Just tell me what you want from me, Cody. If something we do helps stop Tomaso Calderone and his league of hit men and pushers, then I won't be sorry for any of this."

"That's my girl."

MY GIRL. Only she wasn't, and he couldn't let himself start thinking and acting like she was. Even if Sarah was everything she said she was. Even if her motives were one hundred percent pure, she wasn't for him, and he had no business pretending that there could be anything between them. She needed a father for her baby. He was not that man.

He turned back to dry the last two spoons and put them away. An agonizing howl stopped him. He dropped the towel and spoons and raced to the bedroom. His heart plopped back into place when he reached the doorway and saw Sarah standing in the middle of the room clutching her coat to her chest.

He leaned against the doorframe. "You screamed, madam?"

"The disk." She closed her eyes for a second and then opened them as a burst of air rushed from her lungs. "It's missing."

Chapter Eight

Cody stormed into the room, doubts pouncing to the surface then rampaging through his mind. "What do you mean you don't have the disk?"

"It was here, and now it's gone." Her voice rose to a shaky high. The shiny lining of the coat caught the reflection of the overhead light as she held it toward him. "I had sewn a special pouch into the lining, halfway between the pocket and the hem."

"So that's why you held on to that coat as if you were about to be abandoned at the North Pole. You haven't let it out of your sight all day except when you went to the bathroom, and it was in my sight then. If you stashed the disk in the lining, it can't be gone."

She dropped to the bed. "It can't be, but it is. The man who tried to kidnap me must have found it and taken it with him."

"That's impossible. You said yourself, you were standing in the door when he pushed his way in. If he'd found the disk, you would have seen him."

"Then that leaves only you, Cody. You're the only person besides me who's had the coat in your hand. When I went to bed last night, it was on the hanger. When I woke up, it was tangled in the bedcovers."

"You tossed and turned all night and kept kicking your feet out from under that short sheet. I threw the coat over them so you'd keep warm." Cody took the coat from her hands. "The disk must be stuck in the lining somewhere. We may have to rip the coat apart to find it."

"Too late. The early ripper gets the disk." She walked over and lifted the hem, tucking her finger inside a ragged slit. "Someone cut the lining and lifted out the disk. If it wasn't you or the man at the fishing camp, then who could it have been?"

Cody fought the frustration that turned his stomach to a pit of acid. He replayed the events of the morning, knew the man who'd broken into their room and tried to abduct Sarah couldn't have taken the disk. If he'd had it, he wouldn't have been taking Sarah with him. He'd have killed her on the spot the same way he'd killed the night watchman.

He examined the damage. It zigged and zagged just beneath the seam that Sarah had apparently hand sewn into the lining, and part of the tear ran along the bottom edge of the pouch. It must have caught on something and been torn during their trip to the cabin. It could be anywhere.

"When was the last time you put your hand on the disk, Sarah?"

"After the attack in the airport."

"You mean you carried this coat around for two days without even checking to make sure the disk was still in place?"

"Don't go accusing me, Cody Gannon. You're the one who insisted I leave my coat and purse with you every time I went to the bathroom."

"That was to keep you from sneaking away the way

you did at the airport. You should have checked it this morning before we left the fishing camp. You were alone while I went to get the truck. Or you should have checked it during the day.''

''I was a little shaken up this morning, in case you don't remember. It's not every day I have to fight for my life. Besides, if I'd been constantly checking the lining of my coat, you'd have figured out in a minute where it was, and I had no reason to trust you at first. You certainly didn't trust me.''

''Okay, let it go for now. And be quiet a minute. I have to think.''

''I don't know why I have to be quiet. You ranted and raved enough.'' She paced the room and then came back to wag a finger in his face. ''Besides, I did check. Sort of. The bulge of tissue I'd stuffed around the disk brushed against my leg when I walked. I assumed the disk was still there.'' She reached to the bed and picked up a pad of folded tissue and held it up for him to examine. ''You see. The tissue is still there. It was tucked in between the stitches and didn't fall out.'' Her voice wavered and her eyes glistened with unshed tears.

Cody threw up his hands. He couldn't handle tears. His defense against them had always been to walk away, but he couldn't walk away this time. He was in this as deep as Sarah. A seeming accomplice to the theft of the secret files and the murder of the night watch-man.

''Look, Sarah, I'm not blaming you. I just need time to figure this out. I refuse to believe the disk is gone until we've searched every possible spot it might be.''

He spread the coat out on the bed and ran his finger along the lining, inch by inch, stretching the fabric and making sure there were no indentations or rough edges, no places the disk might have fallen and wedged itself in the fabric.

"Let's go look in the truck," she said, when it was obvious he wasn't going to find it in the lining.

"That was my next plan of action, but you can stay inside. It's cold out tonight."

"No problem. I have a *coat*." She picked it up with two fingers as if it was contaminated.

He held it while she shoved her arms into the sleeves. "I'll get a flashlight," he said, heading for the kitchen. "And some tools. I may need to pull the seats loose from the brackets. I doubt we'll find the disk in the truck, but I sure don't want to overlook it if it's there."

She followed him. "I should never have trusted the man who said he was Dan Austin. But he seemed so knowledgeable about everything going on at the DPS. He even hinted to me that the files might prove my new boss had been sneaking secrets to Calderone."

"You never mentioned that before."

"It wasn't important before. Do you think that might be the case?"

"I doubt it."

"Why? It makes sense, you know. As soon as Cochran took over the job, there was a big botch-up with a drug bust around Eagle Pass. It was as if Calderone knew exactly when we were going to strike. Two border patrol officers were killed in the shootout. That was the main reason I believed Dan Austin when he came to me and asked for my help. I never really trusted Mr. Cochran anyway. He has the look of a traitor about him. His eyes are too close together and he leers at me when he thinks I'm not looking."

"Looks can be deceiving." But Sarah did make a

PLAY "LUCKY 7" AND GET
THREE FREE GIFTS!

HOW TO PLAY:

1. With a coin, carefully scratch off the silver box at the right. Then check the claim chart see what we have for you — **2 FREE BOOKS** and a gift — **ALL YOURS! ALL FREE!**

2. Send back this card and you'll receive two brand-new Harlequin Intrigue® novels. The books have a cover price of $4.25 each in the U.S. and $4.99 each in Canada, but they a yours to keep absolutely free.

3. There's no catch. You're und no obligation to buy anything. charge nothing — ZERO — your first shipment. And you do have to make any minimum numb of purchases — not even one!

4. The fact is thousands of readers enjoy receiving their books by mail from the Harlequ Reader Service®. They enjoy the convenience of home delivery...they like getting the be new novels at discount prices, BEFORE they're available in stores...and they love their *He to Heart* newsletter featuring author news, horoscopes, recipes, book reviews and much mor

5. We hope that after receiving your free books you'll want to remain a subscriber. B the choice is yours — to continue or cancel, any time at all! So why not take us up on o invitation, with no risk of any kind. You'll be glad you did!

YOURS FREE!

PLAY LUCKY 7 FOR THIS EXCITING FREE GIFT!

*THIS SURPRISE
MYSTERY GIFT
COULD BE
YOURS FREE WHEN
YOU PLAY*

LUCKY 7!

Visit us online at
www.eHarlequin.com

NO COST! NO OBLIGATION TO BUY!
NO PURCHASE NECESSARY!

The Harlequin Reader Service® — Here's how it works:

Accepting your 2 free books and gift places you under no obligation to buy anything. You may keep the books and gift and return the shipping statement marked "cancel." If you do not cancel, about a month later we'll send you 4 additional novels and bill you just $3.57 each in the U.S., or $3.96 each in Canada, plus 25¢ shipping & handling per book and applicable taxes if any.* That's the complete price and — compared to cover prices of $4.25 each in the U.S. and $4.99 each in Canada — it's quite a bargain! You may cancel at any time, but if you choose to continue, every month we'll send you 4 more books, which you may either purchase at the discount price or return to us and cancel your subscription.

*Terms and prices subject to change without notice. Sales tax applicable in N.Y. Canadian residents will be charged applicable provincial taxes and GST.

good point. He'd known one of the men killed in that fiasco, but he'd never tied it to Cochran.

"Now if the man had suggested it was my previous boss," she continued, "I'd have never gone along with him. Grover Rucker was totally honest and a jewel to work for."

"The man impersonating Daniel Austin knows a lot more than anyone outside the top realm of the DPS should know. He suggested to me that the leaks might be coming from Texas Confidential, possibly even Mitchell Forbes. Apparently he told each of us what he thought would make us buy into his scheme to steal the files."

"Ohmigosh." She brushed her hair back from her face in a frenzied motion. "I hate to even think about what information I might really have stolen."

"Something Calderone is dying to get his hands on, or rather *killing* to get his hands on."

"While the real Dan Austin is probably turning over in his grave," she murmured. "He was loyal to the core."

"Yeah. A lawman's lawman. Only, I would have sworn that was him I was talking to that night in the bar. The voice, the mannerisms, even his eyes."

Flashlight and Mitchell's small toolbox in hand, Cody pushed out the door. The night was pitch black, the sky leaden with rolling clouds. The wind was out of the north, not frigid like it would be in a few months, but cold enough to sting his eyes and whip at his clothes.

It howled through the mountains, like a woman crying. After the day they'd had, it was enough to set his nerves on edge.

"Do you think the man who followed us last night will find us again?" Sarah asked.

Fear had crept into her voice. Evidently the blackness and the ghostly wails of the wind had gotten to her as well. "We're as safe here as we would be anywhere."

"That is *not* what I wanted to hear."

"Would you prefer a lie?"

"Yeah. A really good one, like, 'You don't need to worry about a thing, Sarah. You're as safe up here as you would be back home in your own bed.'"

"Much safer. I'm here, and you can count on me."

"Okay, cowboy. My baby and I will hold you to that."

A crazy promise he'd just made. No one had been able to count on him before. So why should Sarah be any different? But he would keep her safe from a killer or die trying.

DAN AUSTIN hunkered down, holding close to the fire he'd built of twigs and dead limbs. He could see the light in the cabin, knew that Cody was there with Sarah Rand. They had the benefit of a roof over their heads, a hot shower, a bed to sleep in.

Only he doubted Cody would get much sleep tonight. A man on the run seldom slept soundly. They always knew that danger was only a step behind them. Death was only a heartbeat away.

He pulled his ratty coat tighter and ran his fingers through his fake hair. He wouldn't get too much sleep himself tonight. He had work to do. Dirty, unpleasant work. But the rewards were worth it.

Besides, this was what he did, and he was damn good at it.

CODY LAY AWAKE, staring at the ceiling. The search for the diskette had been futile. He'd practically taken the interior of his truck apart and rebuilt it, a giant puzzle of metal, plastic and upholstery. Sarah had hung in there with him, holding the screws and bolts as he removed them, talking a mile a minute, but not crying again.

Now she was asleep, curled up in the middle of a big iron bed and covered with a worn quilt—at least she had been a half hour ago when he'd gone to bed. Sleeping for two, he guessed. She'd certainly drifted into the snooze stage quickly enough.

Sweet, sexy, *pregnant* Sarah.

When he dived into trouble, he went straight to the bottom. One week, he was part of the Texas Confidential legend, the next he was wanted for questioning in a murder. He was also harboring a fugitive who'd stolen classified files from the Federal Department of Public Safety. A woman he had no real reason to trust, except that his instincts insisted she was telling the truth.

But could he trust his instincts in this case or were they impaired by his crazy attraction to Sarah Rand? Giving up on sleep, he kicked from beneath the sheet and slung his legs over the side of the bed, damning his luck. Or lack of it. If he had the disk, he'd have at least a slim chance of figuring out who wanted the information that was on it and why. As it was, all he had was speculation and dozens of unanswered questions.

He didn't have the disk. Worse, he had no idea where it was. If it had somehow fallen into Calderone's hands and the leak went undetected, it might cost the lives of countless lawmen. If it had been lost at the fishing camp, then the police would surely have it and would have checked out the contents by now. There would be a warrant out for Sarah's arrest, not just for questioning, but for stealing classified information from the DPS. There would be a warrant out for him as well.

He *might* be able to save her from Calderone's hit men. He couldn't save her from the law. And he couldn't do anything about finding out the truth if he was behind bars himself.

He left the room, stalked the hall and then pushed out the back door and onto the wide porch. He could backtrack the day's travels, try to locate every hole in the wall where they'd stopped for food or a bathroom break. Check out every two-pump station where they'd stopped for gas. But even if he managed to find them all, there was little chance the disk would be sitting around waiting on him. The best scenario would put it in some county trash-burning barrel or in a small-town garbage incinerator.

That would also be the worst scenario. It would mean Calderone's men were still after the disk, and they wouldn't give up until it was in their hands or until Cody and Sarah were both dead.

Cody exhaled sharply as a gust of wind rattled the windows of the cabin and drove his T-shirt into his flesh. It had been a night like this the first time he'd come here. The first time he'd met Mitchell Forbes.

Mitchell had been all backslapping and encouraging that weekend. The first meeting of father and son, only Mitchell hadn't bothered to share that fact with Cody, the same way he hadn't bothered sharing it with him when he was a kid and could have used a decent man to turn to.

Big man Mitchell Forbes. So big he walked out on the woman he got pregnant. So big he never bothered to see if Cody was all right or if his mother was happy and safe. So big, he let his son and the woman he'd impregnated live through hell.

All past history. Only the memories remained, and they were all Cody needed to decide that as far as he was concerned Mitchell Forbes no longer existed.

He walked to the edge of the porch and leaned over the railing, listening to the night sounds and telling himself that the hard knot in his chest was not the pain of loss. How could he lose a father he'd never had?

He only wished he could put the man out of his mind.

SARAH PRANCED around a clump of thorny brush and climbed on top of a two-foot high kidney-shaped stone. Cody had wanted to talk after breakfast, but she'd had an early-morning case of cabin fever. The talk could wait, she'd insisted, as she cajoled him into taking her for a walk.

The fresh air and exercise were already taking effect. It was her first time in the mountainous region of West Texas, and she was captivated by the uniqueness of the land.

"I've seen this scene in the movies before. I know I have. All that's missing are the outlaws and the horses." She ducked behind a jagged-peaked boulder and poked her head over the top. Squeezing her eyes shut, she made a pretend gun of her finger and pointed it at Cody. "Hands over your head, cowboy."

"Reckon you better not shoot the man who knows the way out of here," he drawled, tipping his hat in authentic western fashion.

His hair caught the wind, and he brushed his fingers through it before plopping the hat back on his head. Strange how well he fit out here. His boots, jeans, even his manner of walking. Rugged, like the land. A hint of danger, a full helping of excitement. "I'm not sure I want to find my way out."

"You definitely climbed out of bed on the right side this morning."

"I always do. No matter how grim things seem when I go to bed, I open my eyes in the morning, see the sun, and I know everything will work out."

"I wish daybreak was that kind to me."

"You need more faith." She spread her arms and lifted her hands, palms facing the sun. "You have to grab life, Cody, reach out and collect all the good parts, like finding beautiful rocks in the dust." She bent over and picked up a pebble to make her point. Holding it between two fingers, she rubbed it against her pantleg until the layer of dirt fell away and a hint of orange appeared. "See. You never know when you'll find a treasure."

"No. Mostly I seem to find mine fields." He stepped closer and propped one booted foot on a decaying stump. "Did Todd share your optimistic philosophy of life?"

"No. He was practical, at least that's what I told myself in the beginning. Actually, controlling would probably be the better adjective. Controlling and selfish, a real me-first kind of guy."

"Yet you picked him to be the father of your child?"

"It wasn't that clear-cut. I didn't plan to get pregnant. I was taking the Pill, but suddenly my hormones started going haywire, and the doctor told me I had to go off it for a while. I suggested we abstain for a couple of months, kind of regroup and get to know each other on a different level."

"I'm not sure men have that many levels, Sarah."

"For sure, Todd didn't. He said there was nothing

wrong with our relationship, that the problems were all in my head. He promised he'd take care of *everything*."

"So what happened?"

"Unfortunately, his *everything* broke one night."

Cody kicked at a clump of dry earth. "The pregnancy was probably a shock to him. He may have had time to reconsider by now."

"I don't know about Todd, but I have. Reconsidered and regrouped."

"If he came back, would you forgive him?"

"In a New York second. I'd even thank him."

"I don't understand." He looked up and met her gaze.

Awareness sizzled between them, as quick and deep as it had just before he'd kissed her last night. Her chest constricted, and she felt the need to be totally honest with him. "What Todd and I shared wasn't love. It was—familiarity. A mutual dependency. Neither of us wanted to be alone. But I always knew something was missing from the relationship."

"Romance is hard for a man."

"I know, but I'm not talking about sending flowers or buying candy. I'm not even talking about remembering to say I love you." She sat down on the same stone she'd stood on a few minutes earlier and stretched her feet out in front of her. "Trust was missing, that knowledge that he'd always be there for me and that I'd always want to be there for him."

Cody looked away. She'd made him uncomfortable with her talk of love and trust. Yet, she had the feeling he was the kind of man who was as enduring as the land he seemed so much a part of. If and when he ever fell in love, the woman he chose would be a very lucky woman.

He kicked at a clod of dirt. "I think we should go back to the cabin."

"I'd rather talk out here. I like the feel of the wind in my face."

Cody stared into the distance, avoiding eye contact. She watched him and had the uneasy feeling he was putting off telling her something. She couldn't imagine what new complication could have developed overnight. Still, the metallic taste of dread filled her mouth and made it hard to swallow. Thoughts of romance and trust vanished. "You're awfully transparent," she said.

"Meaning?"

"You have bad news. Did you talk to the fake Daniel?"

"No. He hasn't called again."

"Then what is it?"

He walked over and placed both hands on her shoulders, finally meeting her gaze again. "I've given the lost diskette a lot of thought."

"I did, too. I have this feeling that it fell out of my coat at one of the stops we made yesterday. It's probably just lying around, kicked under a table or smashed by a car."

She was doing it again. Babbling. Too nervous to stop. Too afraid to hear what Cody had to say. "We could retrace our path," she continued, "stop every place we stopped yesterday. I'll bet we find it in that hamburger joint where the waitress dropped the plate of French fries on the floor."

His finger dug into her flesh. "Don't, Sarah. Please, just listen."

"Okay." The word was a whisper. "But I know from the look on your face that I'm not going to like what you have to say."

"I don't like it myself." His hands left her shoulders and rode up and down her arms. "We have to act on the theory that the files are in Calderone's hands. It's too risky not to. We can't pretend that innocent lawmen won't be killed because of information found on the disk, maybe even my friends with Texas Confidential."

"But the disk could be anywhere. If we look, we may be able to find it."

"It won't work, Sarah. We can't retrace the route we took yesterday. If we try, it's almost certain we'll get picked up by some branch of the law. There will be roadblocks by now and our pictures will be in every police and sheriff's station across the state. It will go better on you if we go to the DPS and report what you did. You can explain your motivation."

"Explain how I spied on my boss and picked up his secret password. Explain how I stole classified information. They'll snap the handcuffs on me before I finish the first sentence."

"We'll get you a lawyer."

"The kind I can afford wouldn't be able to get me out of a jaywalking charge." She clasped and unclasped her hands. "The last thing I want is for any more innocent people to get killed, Cody. I couldn't bear that on my conscience. But isn't there still a chance that the man who asked me to deliver the files really is Dan Austin? We could go to him and try to find out."

He dropped to the rock beside her and wrapped his arm about her shoulders. "He's not the man he claimed to be, Sarah. If I believe him, then I have to accept that you are the traitor, that you were selling out to Calderone for a million dollars in unmarked bills."

"Why do you believe me, Cody?"

"Because if the operation was as straightforward as

the man put it to me, no one would have attacked you at the airport. No one would have followed us to the fishing resort.''

"Then it's not me you believe but the facts."

"That's not entirely true. I could probably explain away some of them." He leaned in closer, his lips a hairbreadth away from her ear. "If I don't believe you, I have to doubt every lawman's instinct I've come to trust."

"Thanks."

"I haven't done anything to thank me for."

"Oh, yes, you have. You can talk facts all you want, but the bottom line is you believe in me. That matters more than you'll ever know. But, you're right. No matter that my intentions were good, I did the deed. Now I'll have to face the punishment." She turned away, heartsick. "I wanted to be the perfect mother. I dreamed of holding my baby, singing her lullabies, kissing away her tears. None of that will happen. My baby will be born to a convicted felon, inside prison walls."

Cody folded her in his arms, pressed her head against his chest with the palm of one hand while he ran his fingers through her hair. "Your baby will be born to a mother who loves her. That already puts her ahead of the game."

She stayed in Cody's arms until her pulse steadied and her will grew stronger. Then, hand in hand, they started down the mountain and back toward Mitchell Forbes's cabin. The air was still fresh, the sun still bright. Only her mood had changed. She struggled against the overpowering odds that tried to pull her under. She couldn't give up hope. She had her baby to think of.

Glancing to the west, she spotted a flutter of wings

and a group of birds circling just over the tops of some scrubby trees a few yards to their left. She watched for a second and then pointed in their direction. "They look like fighter pilots about to attack."

"You *are* a city girl. Those are buzzards circling their breakfast. Probably a dead squirrel or rabbit. Could even be a coyote."

The thought of the dead animal twisted in her stomach, a reminder that her digestive system was not quite back to normal. She stayed lost in her own thoughts until they neared the cabin.

They reached the clearing, and Cody tugged her to a stop. "Looks like we have company."

She spotted the truck then, parked behind Cody's. "I thought you said no one would find us here."

"Goes to show I'm not fail proof."

"What do we do?"

He fished in his pockets and pulled out his key ring. "I want you to take these and go to the truck," he said, pressing the keys into her hand. "If you see anyone besides me come out of the house, I want you to floor the accelerator and get out of here. Go somewhere and call the Smoking Barrel. Ask to speak to Rafe Alvarez and then tell him everything. He'll get you to the DPS."

She hooked her arm though his. "I'd rather go inside with you."

"Just this once, can you do what I ask you without an argument?"

"All right, but I don't know why I should go to Rafe Alvarez. I don't even know him."

"I do. He's a friend of mine. You can trust him with your life." He took her hand, squeezed it, then let go all too soon. She hurried to the truck, hating the feeling of being all alone as she watched Cody take his gun from the shoulder holster. Afraid for him as much as for herself.

She cringed as the screen door to the cabin squeaked open and then slammed shut behind him.

Chapter Nine

Cody stepped inside the back door of the cabin. Mitchell's latest guest was at the table, drinking coffee and munching on the biscuits and bacon left from their breakfast. The acrid odor of boiled coffee hung heavy in the air.

"I'd say make yourself at home," Cody said, "only it looks like you already did."

The man looked up and grinned. "Sorry for barging in. I didn't expect to find anyone else here this time of the year. Season's not open on anything, as far as I know, unless it's quail or wild turkey. I never hunt birds myself."

"I'm not here to hunt."

"Me, either. I started to leave when I saw the truck, then decided to wait around and see if Mitchell was up here."

"He's not." Cody scrutinized the man as he walked over to the table. Middle-aged, fiery red hair, thin brows and moustache, fat lips, big ears. And probably not nearly as innocent as he was trying to sound. "I didn't catch your name."

"Peter Rucker." He extended his hand. "My father is Grover Rucker. He's a friend of Mitchell's. Actually they work together, at least they did until my father retired a few weeks ago.''

''Would that be Grover Rucker with The Federal Department of Public Safety?''

''One and the same. Mitchell's had us up here several times to hunt, so when I realized I'd be working out this way, I came a couple of days early. Thought I'd catch up on my reading and do some hiking.''

''What kind of work do you do?''

''I'm a geologist with Milton and Grange. You've probably heard of them. Anyway, we're doing some preliminary studies for an oil company.'' He downed a gulp of his coffee. ''I hope you don't mind my finishing off your leftovers, but I missed breakfast and that bacon looked too good to pass up.''

''Don't mind a bit.'' Cody spun the nearest chair around and straddled the seat, resting his elbows on the backrest. ''How did you get in?''

''The front door.''

Cody's guard spiraled up another rung or two. He was certain he hadn't left the door unlocked and he seriously doubted that Sarah had.

''I used this key.'' Peter pulled a key from his pocket and tossed it onto the table. It bounced a couple of times, then slid across the smooth wooden surface. ''Mitchell always leaves a key taped to the bottom side of that rocker out there. I accidentally carried this one off with me the last time I was here.''

''You sound as if you come here often.''

''Mitchell said to come up anytime, so I take him up on it when I'm out this way.''

''That's right generous of Mitchell.''

''I don't think you mentioned *your* name,'' Peter

said, wiping crumbs from his chin with the cuff of his sleeve.

"Bill Johnson." It was as good a lie as any.

"Glad to meet you, Bill, and thanks for the breakfast."

Cody glanced toward the back door. He knew Sarah would be worried, but he didn't want her involved in this discussion. She tended to talk too much and he didn't want to give anything away until he knew if Peter was telling the truth about his reasons for his unexpected visit. "I need to check on something outside. Have another cup of coffee. I'll be back before you finish it."

"What the hell?" The man jumped up from the table and grabbed his gun, pointing it at the back door.

Cody jerked around in time to see what had set the man into orbit. The shadow of an arm extended along the open back door, a hammer clutched in the hand, poised for attack. He jumped up and pushed the man's gun hand to the side. "Get in here, Sarah, and you can put the hammer down."

Sarah stepped inside. "It had been almost ten minutes. I thought you might need my help."

He glared at her. "I love the way you follow orders."

She ignored the comment and turned to stare at their guest.

Peter grinned. "That's the way it is with women these days. They don't want their husbands telling them what to do. But since you're here with your little woman, I know you don't need my company." He stood and shoved his arms back into the jacket he'd left hanging on the back of his chair.

Sarah rounded the table and stood across from him,

rolling her hand over her stomach. "I'm not particularly little, and he's not my—"

Peter waved a hand to cut her off. "You don't have to explain anything to me. I'm just passing through. I thank you for the leftovers and if you'll let me borrow your bathroom, I'll be out of here before I cause any more hard feelings."

"The bathroom's down the hall." Cody waited until the man left the room and then filled Sarah in on what had happened, keeping his voice low.

"Mr. Rucker does have a son named Peter," she said, when Cody explained the identity of the man. "I've never met him, but there was a picture of him in Mr. Rucker's office and that man looks a lot like the photograph. But why is he here?"

"He claims he was just in the area and stopped by, that Mitchell extended the open-door policy to him and his father."

"Way out here? This is not a drop-by kind of place."

"Not unless you're a snake or a coyote."

"Do you think the DPS sent him?"

"That's doubtful since he doesn't work for the DPS, at least not that he's admitted."

"So what are you thinking?"

"That the man who claimed to be Dan Austin looked a lot like an elderly drunk the night I ran into him in the bar."

Sarah fell to the chair, propped her elbows on the table and buried her head in her hands. "You surely don't think this is the same man in another disguise?"

"I'm not ruling out the possibility."

"I know Dan could make himself look like anyone from sixteen to a hundred and six, but I didn't think I'd ever run into anyone else that good."

"I don't know that we have. This could well be Peter Rucker. It just seems awfully coincidental that he'd show up here now."

"But if he's not telling the truth, how did he know where to find us?" She unburied her head and laid her hands flat on the table. "So, what do we do, cowboy?"

"Nothing yet, but..."

He let his whisper fade to silence as Peter Rucker came out of the bathroom and strode back into the kitchen.

"It was nice to meet you two, but I'll clear out of your way and let you get on with your vacation. Tell Mitchell hello for me. And you can tell him Dad hates retirement. I think he misses the excitement, though he claims it's Mom's honey-do list that makes him wish he was back at his desk."

Cody walked him to the door and exchanged final parting comments. Man talk, about hunting and the new dates for bow season. Every movement, every facial expression, every word out of the man's mouth seemed relaxed and natural. Nothing to make anyone believe he was there for any reason except the one he'd stated.

Still, as Cody watched the cloud of dust rise and then settle behind the departing pickup truck, he couldn't shake the feeling that the man was not Peter Rucker.

When he got back to the kitchen, Sarah was standing at the sink, rinsing the man's breakfast plate. "I have a strong feeling about that man, Cody."

"Another funny-colored aura?"

"You can laugh, but I'm usually right. I think that was one of Calderone's men. Which means the man could come stalking back and murder us in our sleep."

"Remind me not to ask you to tell any bedtime stories."

She shivered and Cody wrapped her in his arms. He searched for words to try to reassure her. "If the man had wanted to kill us, he wouldn't have been sitting at the kitchen table eating when we returned to the cabin. He'd have been hiding and trying to catch us unaware."

She rested her head on his chest. "I just want to get out of here. I'm ready now to do what you said. Go to the DPS and turn myself in while I'm still alive to do it."

"I just wish I knew what was on those files."

She pulled away enough that she could meet his gaze. "We could always sneak into my Washington office and look them up again."

"I thought you no longer had a copy of the file names."

"I never did. Mr. Austin made me memorize them. Let's see…" She closed her eyes and started typing on an imaginary keyboard. "…s8pqfm9. I know that's the first one I copied."

"Why didn't you say you had the file names memorized when I asked you if you still had them?"

"I didn't trust you then. Besides, up until last night, I thought we had the disk."

"I want to see what's in those files, Sarah. The sooner the better. But we don't have to go to Washington. You should be able to access those files using the computer in the communications room at the Smoking Barrel."

She tilted her head to one side and eyed him suspiciously. "You want me to *break* into Mitchell Forbes's system again?"

"I don't see any other way."

"You are out of your mind. I absolutely refuse to break into a system that belongs to Texas Confidential, especially right under their noses.'' She stood defiantly, hands on her hips. ''No, no, and double no. You have the wrong woman.''

The beeper at Cody's waist vibrated. He checked the number of the caller. The Smoking Barrel. Penny again, he was sure, wanting him to visit Mitchell. This time she might get her wish. He'd like to know about the relationship with Mitchell Forbes and Grover Rucker.

''Work on remembering the file names, Sarah. I want to go into town after lunch. I have a couple of phone calls to make.''

''Forget it, Cody. I'm not breaking into Texas Confidentialfiles.''

''Then I will. All you have to do is give me the names.''

''And leave me here to wait for the man who was here earlier to return, this time in his *Psycho* disguise?''

''Just think about your Mom. I'm sure she has a saying for this, too.''

She stuck her tongue out at him as he exited the room. Weird, but even that turned him on. He had to get this thing over with quickly, before he forgot that this was strictly business. Before he fooled himself into thinking he was capable of commitment, when he knew he didn't have what it took to be a father. Like father, like son. Go for the gusto. Run from the ties that bind. The legacy lived on.

But he and Mitchell would never be father and son. Birth hadn't made it happen. Neither had two years of working together. Now the man was in the hospital, maybe dying. He wished he didn't care, wished the fact wasn't eating away at him like some cancerous sore that wouldn't heal.

He wished it. But his heart knew it wasn't so.

SARAH TWISTED the knob on the radio in Cody's truck, passing up farm and ranch news and a Spanish-speaking station and finally landing on one playing a Garth Brooks number. "There is a serious lack of radio stations in this area."

"That's because there is a serious lack of people."

"I like that part. It's almost as if the two of us are the only people in the world. Come to think of it, this would be a great place for a honeymoon, under other circumstances, of course."

"I didn't think you city girls liked the wilderness."

"City girls don't lump together any more than Texans do."

"I was just making small talk."

"You? Now that surprises me."

"Guess you're rubbing off on me."

Rubbing off on Cody Gannon. The idea was intriguing. Actually it was downright erotic. Heat flushed her skin, and she lowered the window to cool off a bit. "I wouldn't want to be this isolated all the time," she said, when she was sure her voice wouldn't give away the impulses his stray comment had aroused. "But I could handle it occasionally."

They rode in silence until movement in the brush at the side of the road caught her attention. "Did you see that? It looked like a dog or a cat, but what would it be doing out here?"

"It was a fox and I'm sure it has a den nearby."

"It looked too small to be a fox."

"It's a kit fox. They don't grow much larger than that. That's only the second time I've seen one up here. They usually hunt at night. Something must have spurred him out of his easy chair today."

''My first fox outside of a zoo. I'll have great stories to tell Joy one day about our Texas adventures.''

''Joy? I haven't heard you mention her before.''

''Sure you have. I talk about her all the time. I just don't usually call her by name.''

Cody took his eyes from the winding road and glanced in her direction. ''Is Joy your Mom?''

Her mother. A tinge of guilt badgered her conscience, but she let it slide away unheeded. ''Joy's my baby girl.'' She patted her stomach, loving the thought that the fetus was snuggled inside her, growing bigger every day. ''Her real name will be Joycelyn, but I plan to call her Joy. She'll be born in the Christmas season, and she'll bring a world of joy to me.''

''What if Joy is a boy?''

''Maybe I'll call him Cody.''

A smile cracked his lips and then disappeared as quickly as it had appeared. ''I wouldn't.''

''Don't you like your name?''

''I like it fine, for me. I'm just not a fit namesake for a kid.''

''I hope you don't mind if my opinion differs.''

''Suit yourself.''

The lines in his face grew hard and he stared straight ahead. It amazed her that he seemed so cocky, so confident when it came to making decisions and facing killers, but yet he held himself in such low esteem in personal areas.

She wasn't a psychologist, but she'd be willing to bet that someone had let him down really badly in the past. If it was a woman, she must have been nuts.

She slipped her hands behind her neck and leaned against the headrest. It was the pregnancy, she knew, but any time things grew quiet in the afternoon, she found herself fighting to stay awake. "How much farther?"

"About ten miles. Nothing is close out here."

Her eyes grew heavy. She let them close, let her thoughts drift where they would. Killers, files, Calderone, and Cody Gannon. One bright spot in the midst of a horror tale.

She was half in, half out of sleep when she felt it. She opened her eyes instantly and her hands flew to her stomach. It happened again, this time harder, more distinct.

"Pull over, Cody."

"What's wrong?" He didn't wait for an answer. He slowed and pulled to the hard dirt shoulder of the road.

"It's the baby. I felt her kick."

"Inside you?"

"Yes, my baby. Kicking inside me." Her words tripped along her breath, rose with her excitement. "I thought I might have felt her kick before, but this time I know it's real. She's real. Oops, there it goes again, though not as strong this time. Do you want to feel it?"

"I'll take your word for it."

But the moment was too exciting. She wanted to share it with him. Reaching her hand beneath her long shirt, she tugged the waist of her slacks down, revealing a section of her untanned, stretched flesh. "Give me your hand."

He extended it awkwardly. She took it in hers and placed it on her belly, right at the spot where she'd felt the kick. "Be patient," she said, resting her hand on top of his. "Babies don't kick on demand."

CODY FELT the perspiration bead on his forehead. The truck was comfortably cool. The heat was generated by pure panic. He'd never touched a pregnant woman's stomach, never thought about being this close to the beginning of life. He didn't know what Sarah wanted from him, but he was reasonably certain that he wouldn't be able to deliver.

Sarah's flesh dimpled under him, a movement so gentle, he wasn't sure if he'd felt or imagined it.

"Did you feel it? Did you feel her kick?" Sarah's voice strummed across his heart.

"I felt something."

"She's alive." Her voice cracked and wavered. "My own flesh and blood."

Cody looked up to find that Sarah's eyes were moist. He wasn't certain that his weren't as well. His insides were definitely shaky. He wasn't the father of that baby, but he'd felt it kick. His hand on Sarah's stomach. Her hand on his.

"What do you think?" she asked.

He wasn't good with words, never had been. "Amazing. Awesome."

"That's why we have to make it, Cody, why I have to stay alive. Why I have to find out who set me up to steal those files. Why I have to make something good come from my mistake. I have to be a person my baby can look up to. I'm her mother, and I'm all she has."

"She'll be proud of you, Sarah. Even without a father, she'll be one lucky little girl." Cody held Sarah in his arms. He didn't kiss her, didn't touch her in any intimate way. He only held her and yet he was sure he had never felt this close to a woman before.

MITCHELL FORBES sat up in his hospital bed, the faxes Penny had brought him clenched in his hands. He read them again, trying to digest every word and choking on them instead.

Cody Gannon and some fancy-titled secretary at the DPS were wanted for stealing classified information and attempting to sell it to Tomaso Calderone. In the process, they'd reportedly killed a night watchman at some cheap fishing resort and were on the run, probably toward Mexico.

Mitchell slapped the papers against the bed, sick at the words he'd read. Sick of the whole rotten situation. He'd dragged Cody out of one mess after another for as long as he could remember.

Only Cody wasn't a boy now. He was a man, and this time he'd gone and got himself into trouble Mitchell couldn't get him out of.

Mitchell climbed down from the bed and went over to fetch the black briefcase he'd had Penny bring from the ranch. He unzipped the side compartment and rummaged until he found the emergency cigar he'd stuck in there the day before his second heart attack.

He wouldn't light it, but he had to at least poke it between his lips. Tearing the cellophane loose, he dropped the wrapping into the wastebasket and stuck the cigar into his mouth. The taste of it on his tongue was sweet. He savored it, though his thoughts didn't let him find satisfaction.

He walked to the narrow window and stared out on the parking lot. A hell of a way for a man to spend his days. Cooped up in a little, antiseptic-smelling room while his dreams for the future fell apart in his hands.

It had all started years ago when he'd walked away from Rose Wilson—walked away from his son. But he hadn't known what was going on in that house, hadn't known the kind of man Frank Gannon was. Mitchell ran his hands through his thinning hair and down the tight muscles in the back of his neck.

I didn't know, Cody. God help me, I didn't know.

"Mr. Forbes, what are doing with that cigar in your mouth? You know this is a no-smoking room."

The syrupy voice of the nurse startled him. She was his least favorite, though she was cute enough. Nice, perky breasts. Good legs. Aggravating, condescending manner. "I'm not smoking. See, it's not lit." He took it out of his mouth and shook it at her.

"Good. We wouldn't want the doctor getting all upset with us, would we?"

"No. *We* wouldn't."

But right now *he* didn't care. He smiled and made meaningless conversation until the nurse left the room. Then he pulled on his jeans and a worn flannel shirt.

Heart attack or not, he had business that couldn't wait.

Chapter Ten

Sarah roused as Cody brought the pickup truck to a bumpy stop. She looked up but all she saw was more of the wilderness they'd just left. Sparse tufts of long grass, weeds, brush. "Where are we?"

"Still in God's country. A few yards from a two-pump gas station and a ramshackle grocery store."

"Oh, goody, a shopping spree."

"Could be for someone. There's a couple of trucks and a John Deere tractor parked out front. More likely a few of the locals sitting around shooting the breeze and spitting their tobacco in tin cans."

"Sounds like a real hip place." She strained her neck and looked around. "You must be witnessing a mirage. I don't see anything."

"Good, then no one sees us either. Stay in the car. I'll be right back."

"Whoa." She grabbed hold of his right arm while he opened the door with his left. "I'm not too keen on staying by myself these days. Too many surprises. I'll go with you to the pay phone."

"Who said anything about a pay phone? I'm going to *borrow* a cellular phone from one of those parked trucks. He removed her hand from his arm. "And I have a much better chance of not being caught in the act if I'm alone.''

"You can't just take someone's phone without asking, Cody. That's stealing.''

"We're probably wanted in at least forty-eight states. I doubt a stolen phone will hurt our reputation. But, if it makes you feel any better, I'll pay him back when this is over. Now stay put.''

"But those guys might not even have a phone.''

"Then we'll look somewhere else.'' He climbed out of the truck and hiked through a thicket of brush.

She pushed her door open, jumped out and stood by the front fender. She could see the roof of the store now, dark boards without roofing tiles, slanting seriously to the west. The store was downhill from where they'd parked, just off an asphalt road.

Cody disappeared completely behind a cluster of mesquite and then his head popped into view once more before he ducked around the front of the building. Fear slithered up her spine as the isolation closed in around her.

CODY SLUNK between the two trucks. Calling from a phone booth might give away his location, but the origin of a call made from a cellular phone would be harder to pin down. He decided to try the newer truck first, a red pickup with lots of chrome and a gun rack over the back of the seat. A rifle and a shotgun caught the gleam of the sun. Both expensive, but when he turned the handle, he found the door unlocked, just as he expected it would be. A back-roads grocery store in a remote area of West Texas would not be a hotbed for thieves.

Keeping his head low, he easily located the phone

and pulled it loose from the cigarette lighter connection. He backed out of the truck and crept back into the bushes. No one had come in or left the store. No one had stopped for gas. Apparently no one had seen him.

The grass rustled behind him. He turned as a grayish yellow badger scurried through the brush. Better company than a snake or coyote, but Cody didn't linger. He tramped up the hill until he could see the sun shining on Sarah's blond hair as she leaned against the front bumper of the truck.

Satisfied that she was safe, he punched in the number of the Smoking Barrel. The ring seemed interminable. Finally, someone picked up.

"Rafe Alvarez."

Cody hesitated. He hadn't expected Rafe to answer. He'd thought the guys would all be out in the middle of the day and Penny would be the only one around.

"It's your coin, start talking or at least breathing heavy. One of us should get something out of your wasting my time."

"Rafe, it's Cody." He heard the breath escape Rafe's lungs. He could all but see his ex-cohort glaring at the phone. His muscles would be tight as he decided if he was angry Cody called or glad to hear from him.

When he finally spoke, irritation added a scratchy edge to his voice. "Every lawman in this state is on the lookout for you."

"I kind of figured they might be."

"Where in the hell are you?"

"I'm not at liberty to divulge that information right now."

"Don't hand me that crap. You're in deep trouble, partner. You and some pregnant woman. Are you with her now?"

Cody agonized over how much he could say without making things worse than they already were. "I'm with her, but she's not the traitor they're making her out to be."

"Then she better have a damn good lawyer. The both of you had."

"Exactly what is it she's supposed to have done?"

"You should know. Some woman who owns a fishing camp gave a description of the two of you. Said you checked into one of her cabins a couple of nights ago. You were her only guests that night. When she arrived at the camp the next morning, you and *Mrs. Carpenter* were gone and her night watchman was lying in a pool of blood with a bullet in his chest. Dead."

"We were there. We didn't kill the man."

"The police think otherwise."

"And what do you think?"

Rafe muttered a few curses under his breath, but not so low Cody didn't hear them.

"Simple question, Rafe. Do you believe me or not?"

"You're hotheaded, Cody. You wear a chip on your shoulder that's balanced so precariously a man can look at you crooked and knock it off. And you stormed out of here a week ago saying you were quitting the Confidential for good and refusing to give any reason for your actions. But…"

Cody's fingers tightened around the phone. "Just tell me what it is Sarah is supposed to be guilty of and I won't bother you again."

"You didn't let me finish."

"I'd heard enough."

"I'm not through talking. You asked me if I believed you killed a man. The answer is no, not unless you had reason. Not unless you thought he was going to pull the trigger first.''

''I appreciate that.''

''You can't take it to the bank. Every other lawman in the state appears to feel differently right now.''

''What about the other Confidential agents?''

''Naw. Brady and Jake agree with me. You're neither a killer nor a traitor. But you'll need a bulldozer to get yourself out of the hole you're in.''

''I don't suppose you have one handy.''

''Not this time.''

So Brady and Jake believed he was innocent, but Rafe hadn't mentioned Mitchell Forbes and Cody wasn't going to ask. ''What else have you heard about Sarah Rand?''

''This isn't for public consumption, but some undercover agent says he approached her about stealing some files, told her he was one of Calderone's men. He offered her a hundred thousand dollars.''

''Did he say she took him up on his offer?''

''His story is that she acted like she'd never done anything like that before but said she needed the money to take care of her baby. Now she's up and disappeared without the money. He thinks she was the leak all the time and that Calderone warned her to get out before she got caught.''

''Who is this undercover agent?''

''Top secret. No one is releasing his name, apparently to save him from getting on Calderone's hit list before he has time to testify. My guess is he's already been zoomed away to a safe house somewhere.''

''So all they have is his word against Sarah's.''

''No. They have proof that she tampered with the files. She stole not only the ones he'd faked for her to steal, but some authentic, highly classified ones as well. They're not sure how many, but the whole system has been compromised. So has the secrecy of Texas Confidential.''

The revelation added new dimensions to Cody's resolve. Lies, lies and more lies. This was the work of Tomaso Calderone. It smelled of him. Rank, vile, fetid.

A few days ago, news like this might have convinced him that Sarah was guilty, but not now. He'd watched her sleep, heard her laugh, dried her tears, touched her stomach and felt her baby kick. No, this was nothing of Sarah Rand.

And somehow Cody had to prove it before Sarah was arrested and locked behind bars or before Calderone silenced both of them forever. But he no longer had to worry about alerting the DPS that the stolen files were missing. They were apparently on top of the situation.

''Are you still there, Cody?''

''I'm here.'' Only he'd forgotten he still held the phone to his ear. ''Is there more?''

''Just that Penny's been trying to reach you. Mitchell's not doing well. If the odds the doctors are giving him were for a poker hand, he'd have dropped out by now.''

The realization that Mitchell might not make it through the surgery ground in Cody's gut, choked the air from his lungs. Hit him with feelings he wasn't about to deal with now.

''How's Mitchell taking all of this?''

''Hanging tough. Acting like it's no big deal. He's asking for you, though.''

''Does he know about the stolen files and the dead night watchman?''

"You know Mitchell. He knows everything, probably more than any of the rest of us."

"Yeah. I know Mitchell." He probably just wanted to jump Cody's behind about the trouble he was causing.

They said a quick goodbye and Cody called information.

He retrieved the phone number for the hospital and then punched it in. He didn't know what he was going to say when he got Mitchell on the line. He managed to get through to the nurse's station on Mitchell's floor.

"I'd like to speak to Mitchell Forbes."

"Are you family?" The urgency in the nurse's voice set him on edge.

"Yeah. I'm family. Has something happened?"

"I'm afraid so."

His chest constricted as if someone had put a foot on his throat. "Tell me what."

"Mitchell Forbes has left the hospital."

"You mean he was dismissed?"

"Absolutely not. He walked out without telling a soul. If you have any control over him, you should get him back up here at once. His life could depend on it."

"ARE YOU UPSET WITH ME?"

Sarah's voice broke into Cody's thoughts. He threw the log he was holding on the fire and turned to stare at her. She had thrown a worn quilt to the floor in front of the hearth and was stretched out across it, her hands pillowing her head.

"Why would I be upset with you?"

"I don't know, but you've been awfully quiet since you got back from making that phone call to the Smoking Barrel. You're not having second thoughts about what that agent said about me, are you?"

"If you mean, do I think you were trying to deliver that disk to Calderone, the answer is no."

"So, what are you thinking about?"

"Just trying to make sense of this. I'm convinced the man who approached you to steal the files and me to pick you up at the airport wasn't Daniel Austin. I'd decided he had to be one of Calderone's men, but after hearing what Rafe had to say today, I'm more inclined to believe he was the agent who said he offered you the hundred thousand dollars."

"No one offered me that kind of money. I wouldn't have taken it if they had, but I'd remember it."

"And it's still not as much as he told me he offered you. I'm sure he's lying, but he could be covering up for himself or someone else who actually has been leaking information to Calderone."

"He could have told Calderone what he was doing," Sarah said, "and Calderone decided to send the men who attacked me in the airport and at the fishing camp."

Cody shook his head. It still didn't add up. "Why didn't Calderone just wait? If that scenario's correct, he would have gotten the disk eventually."

"But he might have had a reason to bypass his source," Sarah said. "Maybe he didn't want to pay up. Or he might have decided the man knew too much and it was time to drop him."

"In that case, the agent's probably on someone's hit list by now. Calderone doesn't let a man just walk away from his service."

Sarah sat up on the quilt and stared into the fire, her face a study of concentration. "If he goes into witness protection, Calderone would have a much harder time finding him.''

"The bottom line remains the same. If Calderone doesn't have that disk, then he's not going to give up until he gets it.''

"My mother always said that nobody wins all the time. Maybe this will be the time Calderone loses.''

Cody walked over to the leather couch and picked up the magazine Sarah had left there. An adorable baby crawled across the cover. Its hair was blond, its eyes green, but a softer shade than Sarah's. Still, with its cute little nose and pouty lips it looked enough like Sarah that it could have been hers.

His throat tightened and he found it difficult to swallow. If Calderone won this time, then Sarah and her baby would lose. He would not let that happen.

He dropped the magazine to the coffee table. Sarah squirmed and turned to face him. "What, you don't want to read about infants?''

"I could read all the magazines they printed and still not be able to change a diaper. I've never been good around babies.''

"Have you ever been around babies?''

"Not really. I was an only child.''

"Spoiled rotten, huh? But I think you'd be great with children. A baby would soften those rough edges of yours.''

"I like my edges rough.''

She smiled and turned toward him. "I might like them that way, too. Come sit by me. I'll feel a couple of your edges and let you know.''

She was teasing, trying to break through the mantle of aggravation and anxiety he'd crawled under. It was working. He could feel the arousal, her smile and invitation walking over him like seductive fingers.

She lay back on the quilt again, like a cat, stretching and getting comfortable. Or like a woman getting ready for a man. His breath caught in his throat and he had to force himself to breathe normally. "It's not the time or the place for..." For making love. Only he couldn't say the words, afraid that voicing it would rip the gate off the corral. Loose all the needs and urges he didn't want to face.

"Not the time or the place." She repeated his words, only coming from her they sounded lyrical, bewitching. "We're alone in a rugged mountain cabin. Flames are dancing in the fireplace. Danger is lurking all around, so thick there's a chance we might not even live to see the sun come up tomorrow. Or if we do, I might be seeing it from a jail cell."

"Don't talk like that. We're going to beat this thing."

"Okay, I won't talk at all." She patted and then smoothed a spot beside her on the quilt. "Come lie down beside me, Cody."

He felt the tightening in his groin, the shortness of breath. "You don't know what you're asking. I may seem harmless, but I'm still a man."

"Harmless? Cody Gannon, you have a strange image of yourself." Her legs slid across the quilt, her breasts outlined against the knit of her yellow sweater.

Sweat beaded on his brow. "Then let me phrase this differently, Sarah. I'm not made of steel. If I lie down beside you, then I'm going to reach out and touch you."

"And?" Her stare was intense, her eyes emerald pools a man could drown in.

His mouth grew so dry he could barely push the

words past his lips. "If I touch you, I'll want to kiss you. And if I kiss you, I'll want more. I'll want it all."

She reached out to him. "Come lie beside me, Cody." Her words hung in the air, the space between them charged with desire so real he could feel it. He toed the heel of his boot, until his foot slipped out. He shed the other even faster.

A man could only take so much without bursting right out of his skin.

SARAH OPENED her arms and Cody slid inside them. She fought a crazy impulse to laugh, to squeal with delight for what she knew was to come, but she didn't want to frighten him away. "Kiss me, Cody. Kiss me so well that I forget every bad thing that's happened."

"You ask a lot."

"I'll give a lot in return."

He feathered her lips with kisses, quick brushes that set her pulse racing and made her want more. Then he caught her mouth with his. She kissed him back, their breaths mingling, her whole body sucked into the passion. When he finally pulled away, she moaned in pleasure. "Did anyone ever tell you that you are one terrific kisser?"

"Not today."

He caught her bottom lip in his and nibbled gingerly, his fingers riding up and down the center of her breasts. Finally his hands slipped beneath the fabric and trailed her flesh, from her waist up to the lace that bordered the top of her bra. She arched toward him, aching for his touch. Trying to remember if she'd ever wanted a man this way before.

"I never understood why women wear so many clothes."

He tugged on her sweater, and she lifted her body, helping as he pulled it over her head. Her breasts pushed at her bra and spilled over the top. Ample before, they'd blossomed with the pregnancy. Now they tingled in anticipation.

Cody fumbled with the clasp on her bra, finally loosening it to let her breasts spill out and her nipples stand erect. He tossed the bra aside, kissing first one breast and then the other, his tongue caressing the pebbled tips while he cupped their fullness in his strong hands. But then his lips moved from her breasts, trailed kisses up the insides of her arms.

Her body was on fire now, desire so strong she shook with need. Half swallowing new moans of pleasure, she fingered the buttons on his shirt, working until the fabric fell open and she could bury her hands in the wiry mat of dark hairs that peppered his muscled chest.

"Your turn," she whispered, pushing the sleeves down and off his arms. "I'll find spots to nibble you didn't even know you had."

He moaned and caught her lips again. They rolled together, her firm breasts pushing against the hard angular planes of his chest.

She roamed his back with her hands, kissing his earlobes, his neck, the smooth skin of his abdomen. She loved the feel of his body writhing at her touch, loved knowing she was driving him over the edge. Finally, her fingers moved to the zipper of his jeans. She tugged, but couldn't get it to give. "Last one naked is a slimy worm."

"You're on."

But he didn't race her. He helped. Stretching the elastic, he pulled her pants down and over her hips. He stared at the bulge of her stomach, covered only by the silky, see-through material of her panties. For a second, she felt self-conscious about the shape of her body, realized it was the first time she'd been with a man when her stomach wasn't firm and taut.

Cody flattened his hands on her belly, more tender than she would have thought possible from a man so strong. "I've never wanted a woman more, but I don't want to hurt you or the baby."

"You won't." She cupped her hands about the back of his head. "I won't break."

"Is that a promise?"

"A promise." She rolled over to her side and pulled him closer. And then she was lost in the thrill of him as he pushed his way inside her.

Glorious minutes later, passion spent and bodies slick and warm, she lay in his arms and stared into the fire. Twenty-six years old, but she finally knew how real love felt. And for once in her life, she was speechless.

"ARE YOU SURE you want to go through with this, Cody? Walking into Texas Confidential headquarters and logging on to their network sounds like suicide to me."

"No way." He climbed behind the wheel of his truck and yanked the gear into reverse. "Going out the chute on a bucking bronc with murder on his mind. That's suicide. Wrestling a mad steer to the ground. That's asking for trouble. What we're doing is just a night's work for a Confidential agent."

"And if you were still a Confidential agent, I wouldn't be worried."

He reached over and patted her hand, a gesture that did nothing to still her fears. "Trust me. I'm good at what I do."

She couldn't argue with that, especially not after this afternoon. But making love required a very different skill set than walking into an occupied house without being detected. "What if I told you I don't remember the names of the files anymore? Would you call this crazy scheme off?"

"Is that what you want?"

"What I want is for this to be over."

"You can turn yourself in to the police."

"Go to jail for stealing classified information and hope some no-name lawyer can clear me when the deck is stacked against me?"

"That or else wait for Calderone's men to track you down and kill you for a disk you no longer have."

"You can stop now. You've convinced me." She reached behind her and grabbed her seat belt, pulling it down and buckling it in place. "So, let the games begin."

Chapter Eleven

Thankfully the moon was bright, except for the bleak moments when it ducked behind one of the gray clouds that rolled with the wind across the night sky. It illuminated the scrubby brush they had to dodge and the high grass that crunched beneath their boots and rustled with the movement of night creatures Sarah didn't even want to think about. "You didn't mention that we would be on foot for a mile."

"It's hard to arrive unannounced if you drive up in my pickup truck. My motor hasn't purred quietly for the last thirty thousand miles. Besides, this is more like a hundred yards."

"Are there snakes out here?"

"Snakes, lizards, scorpions, tarantulas, woodrats. Take your pick."

A shudder slithered along her spine. "And I thought the streets in D.C. were dangerous at night."

"Most of the nocturnal creatures out here are more afraid of you than you are of them."

"Care to put a bet on that?"

Sarah stopped short, catching her breath at the sound of wings flapping overhead. A large bird flew past them and into the branches of a scrubby mesquite. She breathed again and kept walking, staying close to Cody's heels.

Cody stopped behind a thick wedge of rock. A barb-wire fence cut through the land just in front of them, separating them from a cleared area and then the house.

The house was imposing, two-story, white with a wide porch along the front and sides. Large windows flanked the entrance and two trucks and a Jeep Wrangler were parked outside.

She took a deep breath and exhaled slowly, trying to get up the nerve for what they were about to do. "How many people live here?"

"Mitchell, of course. He has a private suite on the west side of the second floor. Penny's room is right across from his."

"She's the woman who called you the other night at the fishing camp?"

"Right. She's the girl Friday around here. Then there's Rosa, the cook. Makes the best homemade tortillas you'll ever bite into."

"What about the other agents? Where do they live?"

"Some of them live here, but it's not a requirement. Jake has his own small ranch nearby. He and his wife Abby are building a new house on it." He took her hand. "Why the sudden interest in living arrangements? You're not stalling for time, are you?"

"No. I'm thinking of all the reasons this isn't going to work. Even if Mitchell Forbes is in the hospital, this place is crawling with people. There is no way we're going to just walk in, log on to the computer, check a few files and walk off without being detected."

"Mitchell's not in the hospital anymore."

"When did you find that out?"

"This afternoon. I called the hospital from the cell phone."

"You didn't mention that to me."

"I didn't see any reason to."

"Does that mean his condition has improved?"

"No, it means he walked off. He likes giving orders, not taking them." Cody put an arm about her shoulder. "Forget Mitchell and everybody else. You have enough to think about now. Once we leave this clearing, there won't be anything to block us from the view of the house. I want you to move fast and quietly. Stay right behind me, and don't talk."

The moment of truth. Her feet froze to the spot, her heart beating like crazy. There would be little chance they could pull this off, especially with Mitchell Forbes on the premises. They'd be caught. She'd be carted off to jail, a common criminal, her wrists bound by metal cuffs.

If she didn't go with Cody, if they didn't find some clue as to who had set her up and why, then she'd eventually be caught anyway. Or killed. At least this way she had a chance.

"If something happens, Cody. I mean if I were to be apprehended tonight, or worse—I just want you to know that I appreciate your standing by me. You're the first person who ever has."

The breath left his lungs in an exasperated sigh. She knew that emotions were hard for him to deal with, but she had to let him know how she felt. He touched his lips to hers, hard, reassuring, passionate. He was a man of action, more comfortable with doing than with talking. But she knew the kiss was his way of saying he understood what she was trying to tell him.

A cowboy lawman. If anyone could help her now, it

was Cody Gannon. "I'm ready," she said when she'd caught her breath from the kiss. "Lead the way."

CODY SLID HIS KEY into the back door lock. It fit easily, as he was sure it would. No one would have bothered to change the lock on his account. They would never expect him to show up here, the same way they'd never expect him and Sarah to be hiding out in Mitchell's hunting cabin.

They shed their boots and he eased the door open. The predictable creak sounded like fireworks to his ears, but he knew from his two years of living here that the sound wouldn't alert anyone. The old house creaked and groaned all night long, even when no one was up and about.

He tiptoed down the wide hall, Sarah right behind him. A strip of light peeked from beneath the kitchen door. He paid it no mind. Rosa always left the light on over the range. Kept her from banging her toes when she got up in the morning to start breakfast, she claimed, but Cody had always suspected that she just hated a dark house.

He kept to the center of the hall, less chance for them to bump into anything or to brush against one of the pictures on the wall. Slow and easy, one step at a time, all the way to the front of the house and into the library.

He stopped at the row of identical bookshelves on the far wall filled with copies of Mitchell's favorite authors, from Shakespeare to Elmer Kelton.

Stooping low, he pulled out the appropriate book and pushed the hidden button. The bookcases separated, revealing the secret elevator that would take them to the communication center in the basement. This was the only entry, and Penny was the only nonbonafide member of Texas Confidential who knew how to access the elevator. When he turned back to Sarah, her mouth and eyes were open wide.

Grabbing her hand, he tugged her into the elevator, waiting until the door was safely shut behind them before he spoke. "So far, so good."

"A secret elevator inside the musty library of a century-old ranch house. All the adventure I ever wanted and I'm too nervous to appreciate it."

"You can never so much as utter a peep about any of this."

"I know."

"I mean this, Sarah." He held on to her hand while the elevator came to a jerky stop. "You can never talk about the elevator or the room we're about to enter. Not even to your mother."

"You can trust me. I may have broken the cardinal DPS rule when I copied those files, but, believe me, I've learned my lesson."

The elevator doors opened and they stepped out. "Mitchell's computer is the one on the big pine desk in the center of the room," he said, already moving toward it. "I don't know much about technical networking, but I know he can directly access files and information from databases at the DPS office in Washington and in Austin."

"Then I should be able to log on to the top-level classified directory using my boss's password—unless he's changed it."

"Why would he?"

"He may have guessed that was how I broke into the files before."

"Give it a try."

She walked past him and took the swivel chair in front of the screen. One punch and the monitor lit up. A few seconds later and she'd moved from the screen saver to a C-prompt. He stood over her shoulder, willing her to locate the files.

She typed in a cluster of letters and numbers that appeared on the screen as a series of asterisks. "Damn." The word was whispered, but her hands were shaking. "The program doesn't recognize the password."

"Try it again. Maybe you were nervous and keyed in the wrong symbol."

Stretching her fingers over the keys, she took in a deep breath and then typed again. The same message appeared.

He laid his hands on her shoulders. "I should have known this was going too well."

"Since we're here, I may as well try a minute longer, see if I can come up with his new code."

"How would you know where to start?"

"Well, the first one wasn't all that imaginative. It was the letters in his wife's name—backwards—interspersed with the date of his anniversary."

"Sounds pretty creative to me. How did you know the numbers were his anniversary?"

"I made the dinner reservations when they went out to celebrate, and I have a good memory for dates and symbols in a sequence. That's how I'm still able to come up with the file names."

"It's worth a try." Cody's hope bounded and then began a slow plunge as each series of symbols met with the same discouraging message. He paced while Sarah typed and the window of time they had left grew shorter and shorter. Rosa would be up at five-thirty to make coffee and start breakfast. Mitchell would be up by the time the coffee was hot and Penny Archer would be right behind him. The schedules of the others varied.

"It's up."

Cody spun around as the monitor screen changed. "Does that mean you discovered the password?"

"That's what it means. It was the name of his son's soccer team and his wife's birthday. Now if I can just remember the file names with all these new letters and numbers parading through my mind." Excitement colored her voice. Cody moved in closer.

The first file appeared on the screen. A meeting date, time, people in attendance. He blew a blast of hot air from his lungs. "That's nothing but a rehash of a meeting that was held last fall. There's nothing in there Calderone would kill for."

"Maybe it's the names he wants."

"If he wants those names he can just have one of his local *hombres* call DPS. Those are the administrators, available to any U.S. citizen. Pull up another file."

The next file was just as futile. A budget for a conference that was held in Austin last year.

Sarah stretched her fingers. "These must be the fake files the agent said he planted for me to steal. That may be all I ever had. He could be lying about my stealing strategic files."

"All of this to set you up." Cody rubbed his temples.

Sarah spread her hand across the bulge beneath her loose shirt. "I'm going to jail for stealing files that should never have been labeled as classified. I'm giving up my baby for a batch of meaningless information."

"Two people tried to kill you. There has to be more to it than this, Sarah. Try another of the files."

Ten minutes later, they hit pay dirt.

Sarah ran the cursor down a file that appeared jumbled, the letters thrown on the page in random fashion. "It looks like some kind of code," she said, moving her head to the side so that he could get a better look.

Cody stared at the screen, adrenaline pumping as the pieces of the puzzle slid into much better perspective. "It is a code, the one the DPS just devised for use when they're setting up undercover drug strikes. It's fresh off the planning table, never even been used." He ran the cursor down the page. "The code and the names of the undercover agents in each area. If Calderone had gotten his hands on this without the DPS knowing it, Texas Confidential and every other undercover drug agent in the state would have been walking targets."

"And I was the messenger who was going to lay the code in Calderone's hands?"

"If things went well, Calderone would have the disk. If the operation was botched, you would go to jail in place of the real leak, the man who'd been selling information to Calderone in the past. The man who could keep selling information in the future."

"Only why the attack? Why didn't the person who set this up just wait for me to deliver the disk?"

"He was probably afraid you were setting a trap for him. If he met you at the appointed place and time, the DPS would have him."

"I still don't understand. If I was working with the DPS to set a trap for him, the DPS would already know everything. If he killed me or stole the disk, they'd change the code."

"But if you were doing this in secret because you believed the man was really Daniel Austin..."

"Which I was—"

"Then he'd attack you, take the disk, and no one would be the wiser. If he killed you in the process, all the better. That way you'd never suffer the pangs of guilt and squeal."

She ran her hands through her hair and then nervously pushed the mussed strands behind her ears. "But why did he choose you to work with me? And why did he need me at all? If the man had access to the file-names, why didn't he just steal the files himself?"

"We can't solve that part of the riddle now." He handed her an unused disk from the box on Mitchell's desk. "Copy that file and then log off. We may need it."

"Never. I made that mistake once, but never again."

"You have to. I'm not sure how we're going to prove your innocence in all of this, but we may need that file." He stalked the room while she worked, a plan formulating in his mind. One last chance to catch Tomaso Calderone. He chose a few tools of the trade, dropping them into a large brown envelope.

Sarah logged off the computer and he dropped the new disk into the envelope with his supplies. On his way to the elevator, he picked up a cellular phone that one of the agents had left recharging. They'd probably cut off the service when they realized it was missing, but he might get some use out of it before they did.

"Mission accomplished," Sarah announced, as they stepped into the elevator. "Now all we have to do is get out of here without being caught."

By the time they'd reentered the library, the moon

had disappeared behind the clouds, and the room had grown much darker. Silently they maneuvered the hallway, not stopping until they reached the back door.

The inside stairs creaked. Cody jerked around and saw Rosa silhouetted in a frame of light that spilled out of her open doorway.

"It's okay, Rosa. I just came to get some of my things."

"No. *Vayase.* Kill *hombre.*"

"It's all a mistake, Rosa. *Un error grande.* You know me. I wouldn't kill anyone."

He started up the steps. All he wanted to do was reassure her, but he caught the look of panic on her face and knew she was about to scream. Acting on impulse, he planted his hand over her mouth to silence her.

She kicked at his shins, her bob of black hair bouncing on top of her head, her large breasts heaving beneath the cotton housedress. His grip tightened. He didn't want to hurt her, but if she screamed, Mitchell and the others would come bounding down the steps. He had to keep her quiet.

"Go outside, Sarah. I'll catch up with you."

"You can't hurt her, Cody. Please don't hurt her."

Her words cut into him like a jagged glass on an old wound. He'd said those same words before, pleaded, begged that the man he thought was his father not squeeze his mother's neck. Not plant his fist into her face. Not grind his heel into her stomach.

"I don't like the way you're looking at me, Cody. You're frightening me. You're hurting the woman."

He dropped his hand from Rosa's mouth. "I didn't mean to hurt you, Rosa. I didn't. But please don't yell. Just give us a chance to walk away without the others knowing we were here. I didn't kill anyone and neither did Sarah.''

Rosa started to cry and mutter words in Spanish he didn't understand. He skidded down the steps and yanked the door open, all but pushing Sarah out it.

''Stop or I'll shoot.''

The voice came from behind him, spoken without a trace of Rosa's accent.

Chapter Twelve

Cody turned and stared at the woman wielding the gun. For a minute he thought his eyes were playing tricks on him. The woman standing at the top of the staircase looked different, softer, more feminine than he was used to. Her brown hair fell loose about her shoulders and she wasn't wearing her glasses. And instead of the tailored denim skirts and jeans he was used to seeing her in, she was wearing red silky pajamas. They weren't revealing, but they definitely didn't look like anything he'd ever seen her in before.

Her looks gave him courage. "You won't shoot, Penny. I doubt you know how."

"Think again." She waved a small metal pistol in the air in front of her. "Rafe's been giving me shooting lessons, just in case I'm the one who runs into the rustlers."

"We're friends. You don't shoot your friends."

"Friends answer your pages and call you back. Friends don't just walk away without giving explanations."

"My reasons for leaving didn't concern you."

"Yeah, well they do now. You're all over the news

these days. I find that more than enough reason for me to be concerned."

And she'd be even more upset if she knew he and Sarah had just come from the communication center. He had to make sure she didn't find out. "I only came by to get some of my things, Penny. I have them now, and if you'll stop waving that gun around, Miss Rand and I will be on our way."

"You came back for the Christmas cards, didn't you? The ones that little girl you saved from the bank robbers sends you every year."

"That's right," he said, jumping on the excuse she'd thrown him. "I have them right here." He lifted the brown envelope and hoped she wasn't going to demand proof of the contents. "Sarah and I will get out and you can go back to bed." He took a step toward the door.

"Not so fast, Cody. We have lots to talk about." She nodded to Rosa. "Go make some coffee and when it's ready, serve us in the parlor."

"*Si, senorita.* Make tortillas, too. Our Cody is *muy flaco* since *el* Smoking Barrel. *Demasiado* trouble."

"Don't worry about *our* Cody. He'll probably get a lot skinnier when they lock him up in jail."

Rosa shuffled away, her house shoes flopping on her feet, her shoulders slumped, leaving her dress to bulge around her short, pudgy frame. She turned back to stare at them. "No kill him, senorita. He not hurt me."

As soon as Rosa was out of sight, Penny lit into Cody again. "What in the devil is going on? And don't give me any of your wisecracks about how I'm better off not knowing. I've had it up to here with you macho guys and your secrets. You, Mitchell, the rest of the agents. All of you deciding on your own that I'm not *man* enough to hear the truth. But I'm woman enough to run circles around the lot of you.''

Cody had seen Penny aggravated lots of times, but he wasn't sure he'd ever seen her this upset. He eyed the finger that rested on the trigger and decided it was not the time to argue. ''What do you want to know?''

''Everything. Turn slowly and walk into the parlor. You too, Miss. I want to see your hands at all times.''

''My name is Sarah Rand, not Miss.''

The words were spoken like a challenge. Once spoken, she straightened her back, tilted her chin up defiantly and stared at Penny. Cody watched the nonverbal interchange between the two women. One, his friend, the other his…

His what? Lover? Partner in crime? All he knew was that she had become all important to him.

Penny walked down the steps, the gun still pointed at Cody. ''Look, Sarah Rand, I don't know what's going on with you and Cody. I don't know if you dragged him into this mess or if he dragged you into it, but you're both wanted by the police and unless you can come up with an extremely convincing story in record time, I'm about to pick up the phone and call the sheriff.''

''A chance.'' Sarah said, as she linked her arm with Cody's. ''A chance is all we're asking.''

Cody and Sarah led the way to the parlor and Penny motioned them to the oversize leather sofa that faced the fireplace. ''Start talking, Cody. To me or the sheriff. Your call.''

He knew that he could probably jump Penny and take the gun away from her. He'd done it before with men twice her size, but there was no guarantee the gun wouldn't go off in the scuffle. If it did, someone could take a bullet.

"It's a long story, Penny, with more twists and turns than a rodeo clown."

"And you're the one the bull is about to stomp into the ground. Start talking."

SARAH ADMIRED Penny's style. Direct. Confident. If the situation were different, they might have become friends. Reaching over, she laid a hand on Cody's knee. "Let me start."

"You don't have to say a thing, Sarah. Even if you're arrested, you can take the Fifth."

She jerked her hand away. "I don't want to take the Fifth. That's what guilty people do. I made a mistake, a really big one. I expect to pay for it, but I don't want to be railroaded into prison while the man who framed me goes free."

Penny leaned in closer. "Are you working for Calderone?"

"The man's a butcher. I'd sooner work for Hades himself." Sarah dived into the story, starting with the phone call she'd received from the man she'd thought was Dan Austin. Cody jumped in from time to time, saying in a few words what it took her dozens to say. Between them, they covered everything except the real reason they'd come to the Smoking Barrel that night.

To Penny's credit, she listened attentively, interrupting only when she didn't understand something. The only time the conversation ceased was when Rosa brought in a tray with a pot of freshly brewed coffee and three large pottery mugs.

By the time the explanations were finished, the coffee was gone as well. Penny laid the gun on the table and screwed her mouth into a scowl. "Where do you think the missing disk is, Cody?"

"I'm hoping the police have it."

"They don't. I heard Rafe and Brady talking. The area around the fishing camp was searched, but nothing was found."

"Then it could be anywhere."

Penny crossed her arms over her chest. "I'm not sure I should tell you this, Cody, but something big is up with the DPS. All the Confidential agents were called out of town for some emergency meeting. Mitchell was in on it, though he should be in the hospital."

"Do you think it has to do with Calderone?"

"That would be my guess, but I don't know anything for a fact. I'm just the office help. I do as I'm told and keep my hands out of the action."

"I wish I had," Sarah said. "I'd be a lot better off now." Except if she hadn't gone along with copying the files, she'd never have met Cody. The memories of the afternoon rushed in on a wave of heat. She felt a blush burn in her cheeks.

Penny didn't seem to notice. She stood and walked over to stand in front of them. "At any rate, I have the feeling all hell is about to break loose. You're part of the Confidential team. You should be helping."

"I *used* to be a Confidential agent."

"You didn't resign officially. As far as Mitchell is concerned, you just took a few days off to cool down from whatever riled you. He's pulled you out of one jam after another for years before you signed on with Texas Confidential. He knows your temper."

Cody's jaw clenched. "What do you mean, hauled me out of trouble?"

"Just that. Don't worry. The other agents don't know about that. I only know because I did the paperwork."

Cody stiffened. "I never asked for his help."

Sarah sensed as much as witnessed the change that came over Cody. It was if he'd become someone else. Someone hard and cold. She pulled away from him, suddenly unsure of what kind of man she'd let into her heart.

"Mitchell looks out for a lot of people," Penny said. "He took me in when my mother died, only because he and my dad were old war buddies."

"He wasn't *my* dad's buddy."

Penny glared at Cody, her hands planted on her hips. "He said he and your mother were friends back before you were born. The man did you countless favors, even took you on as a Texas Confidential, and this is the thanks he gets."

"I don't need his kind of favors."

Penny stuck her face in his. "Well, bully for you, Cody Gannon. You go right through life not needing anyone and see if it makes you happy. And while you do your own thing, Mitchell is out of the hospital, risking his life, probably to clear up this new mess you've gotten yourself into."

The muscles in Cody's arms strained against the sleeves of his cotton shirt. He leaned over, rested his elbows on his knees while his hands fisted, then straightened in rapid succession.

Tension clogged Sarah's lungs. She tried to stand but a stabbing pain shot through her back. She grimaced, but held back the moan that formed in her throat.

Finally snapping from his own misery, Cody turned to her. In an instant, his whole demeanor changed, grew compassionate and tender. "Is something wrong?"

"I'm fine. Just tired."

"You need to turn yourselves in, Cody, before you get arrested. A pregnant woman doesn't need to be on the run. It's not good for the baby."

"Breakfast." Rosa's voice cut through the room. She stood in the doorway, wiping her hands on the tail of a white apron.

"I'm not hungry," Penny said. "I'll take more coffee, though."

Rosa stepped into the room, her gaze moving from Penny to Sarah. "You eat. *Coma. El bebe necesita comida.*" She smiled and her voice took on a soothing lilt. "I fix tortillas. Cody loves *mis* tortillas. *Son deliciosos.*

He stood and put a hand on her shoulder. "You're the woman, Rosa, best cook in town."

They followed her to the kitchen without arguing. And Rosa was right. A pregnant lady and her baby did need food. In spite of everything, Sarah ate two burritos, both crammed with eggs, *carrizo,* beans and cheese. She left off the hot sauce.

But the pain persisted, milder than before, and centered in her lower back. She'd have to very careful from here on out. It was way too early to go into labor.

MITCHELL PUSHED the lunch tray away and settled back against the lumpy pillows of his too-narrow hospital bed. His business was taken care of, at least the part that he could do and he had checked back into this antiseptic prison like he'd promised his boys that he would.

His boys. Brady, Jake, Rafe. They had all been at the meeting in Austin. All present and accounted for—all except Cody. But then Cody was the reason the meeting had been called in the first place.

He looked up as Maddie Wells stepped through his door.

"That plate looks practically untouched," she complained, staring at his tray.

"Because the food is untouchable. And what kind of greeting is that?"

"As good as you deserve. Leaving the hospital without a word to me. You scared me to death."

"I had business to take care of. Besides, you worry about me anyway. I may as well give you a good reason."

She bent over the bed and kissed him on the cheek. "You need to follow the doctor's orders. Not following them before is probably what landed you here again."

"You know what's wrong with you, Maddie Wells?"

"Nothing. Absolutely nothing, but I'm sure that's not what you're about to say."

"You think like a woman. You want to have reasons for what happens. Life's not like that. It just rears back like a horse gone loco and kicks you while you're down."

"My, you're in a pleasant mood this morning."

Actually he was in a horn tossin' mood, and sitting in this hospital while the fight against Calderone was heating up like a brisket on the barbecue grill was not helping matters a dang bit.

It was nice to have Maddie stop by, though. She never failed to light up a room. Fussy as a mother hen, but a whole lot prettier.

And always busy. She was straightening his table now, moving things around, folding his newspapers, putting his magazines in a neat stack. Her long red hair was balled up on top of her head, but wispy tendrils danced about her neck and fell into her face when she bent over the table.

The V-neck yellow sweater she was wearing was one of his favorites. He was sure he'd told her that before—in a weak moment. It showed off her breasts, still nice at fifty-eight. Her legs were nice, too. Shapely. He preferred her in a skirt, but seldom saw her in one. Today was no exception. The gray slacks she was wearing looked new.

She was five feet nine, a good height for a woman, and while she wasn't willowy the way she'd been when she and her late husband Bill had first bought the neighboring ranch, she still had a damn nice figure.

"What brings you into town so early?" he asked when she started thumbing through a magazine instead of coming back to pester him. "You usually don't make it until late afternoon."

"I came in last night when I was going crazy worrying about you. I had dinner with a friend and caught a movie."

The idea bothered him. "A man friend?"

"What's it to you?"

"Nothing. I was just wondering. Someone has to look out after you."

She threw back her head and laughed, a throaty, seductive, genuine sound. He'd always loved the way she laughed, but right now he didn't see anything that amusing.

"I've been a widow for ten years, Mitchell Forbes. And I'm perfectly capable of looking after myself. I'm the most savvy rancher in this part of Texas."

"The *second* most savvy rancher. And judging cattle does not make you an expert in screening men."

"I might not want them screened. I might be looking

for one last wild adventure before I settle into the life of a mature, older woman."

"You're a long way from that. No one who fills out a sweater the way you do is ready for a rocking chair."

"Excuse me. I must have misheard you. That sounded like a compliment."

"You heard right. You're a good-looking woman, and you know it. A little sassy for my tastes, but that's no reflection on your looks or your age."

"Thank you. And, for the record, I had dinner last night with my friend Jerri. Her daughter's expecting. To hear her talk, she's the first woman to ever become a grandmother."

"You wouldn't be envious, would you?"

"A little. It would be nice to have a baby around, someone to spoil rotten and teach to ride. Someone to call me Grandma. No grandchildren might be the worst part of never having children."

Mitchell adopted an expression that he hoped suggested interest in what Maddie was saying. Most of the time he enjoyed their conversations, loved the way she came back at him with her quick wit, but today pressing problems claimed his mind.

"Mitchell. Mitchell Forbes."

"Yeah, right. That Jerri's a card."

"You are not listening to a word I'm saying." She dropped the magazine she was holding onto the stack. "It's Cody, isn't it?"

"It's not looking good for him." He ran his fingers through his thinning hair and reached for his lighter. He fingered it, rolling it over and over. "I don't know how he ever hooked up with Sarah Rand, but he's got himself in deep this time."

"You don't believe he's actually selling secrets to

Calderone, do you? He's impulsive and moody. He's not a traitor.''

"He's a fugitive from justice. He's traveling with a woman suspected of leaking classified information to the enemy. He walked off his job without giving notice. Would you want the job of defending him?''

"I'm sure he has his reasons. I have faith in Cody. You should, too.''

"I *should* have had better sense than to hire him on as a Texas Confidential agent.''

"Don't be ridiculous. Cody's a natural lawman. You said so yourself at least a hundred times.''

"I saw what I wanted to see and closed my mind to what I didn't want to see.''

"That's forgivable. He's your son.''

"He's *not* my son. He's Frank Gannon's boy. Always was. I just happened to be there the night he was conceived. His mother forgot it. I should have too.''

Maddie pulled a chair to the side of the bed. The scrape of wood on tile rode his raw nerves. Everything grated on him these days.

"What did happen between you and Cody's mother? You've never said.''

"Youth. And a war.''

"Did you ask her to marry you?''

"No. I wasn't in the right place for becoming a husband.''

"And obviously you're still not.''

He looked up from his lighter and met her gaze. Her green eyes danced mischievously. "One of these days I'm going to say yes to one of your proposals,'' he said, "and then we'll see who's laughing.''

"You say yes and I'll march you down to the altar so fast you'll never know what hit you. But you'll be the one laughing. At least you'll wake up with a smile on your face. I promise you that.'' She shook her breasts tauntingly.

One of these days he might just put her to the test. If he lived through the surgery. He raised up on his elbows. ''Are you driving back to the Double U today?''

''Not so fast. I'm not ready to change the subject just yet. You never explained what happened between you and Cody's mother.''

''Let it go, Maddie. I'm in no mood for ghosts of any kind today.''

Maddie leaned over and entwined her fingers with his. ''You should tell Cody you're his father, Mitchell. You owe that to him and to yourself.''

''I should never have gotten involved at all. I hired him on and tried to make him a man.''

''He is a man, Mitchell. His own man. You tried to make him into *you,* and that wasn't fair.''

He squeezed her hand. ''You're quite a woman, Maddie Wells. You don't even mince words with a dying man.''

''You, a dying man?'' she scoffed openly. ''You are far too stubborn to check out. You go and die, and those lawman cowboys you have running around the Smoking Barrel will drink your best Scotch. You know you won't allow that.''

The doctor stuck his head in the door. ''I'd like to know how you do it, Mitchell. Every time I come in you have a different beautiful woman up here playing nursemaid. No wonder your heart's having trouble keeping up with you.''

''It's the badge, doc. It gets them every time.'' He didn't bother explaining to Maddie that Penny had been his other female visitor. He was sure the two of them discussed his health on a daily basis.

Maddie joked while she retrieved her handbag and threw it over her shoulder. She said her goodbyes hurriedly but stopped at the door.

"Don't count Cody out, Mitchell. He has good genes." With that, she winked and disappeared into the hall.

The doctor pulled out his stethoscope and approached the bed. "Now that you're back in the hospital, I hope you're ready to let someone else take over your job."

"Absolutely. I plan to lead a stress-free life." And he was expecting the price of beef to triple this year and his calves to be born with his brand already burned into their hide.

SARAH STOOD on the narrow porch of the hunting cabin. Cody had been unusually quiet since they'd returned from the Smoking Barrel. She'd expected him to be elated that their mission was a success, but instead he was moody and withdrawn. The screen door slammed behind her and she knew he'd joined her on the porch. She didn't bother to turn around.

"Are you getting cabin fever again?" He walked up behind her and wrapped his hands around her upper arms.

Her irritation with him melted. She loved being with him, grew excited at his touch. If she felt that way under the current circumstances, imagine how exciting it would be if they actually made it out of this nightmare free and alive.

"I don't have cabin fever. I just thought you didn't want me around. You wouldn't talk to me."

"I was trying to unravel the knots. There has to be

a reason why the person picked you out of all the other possible employees. And a reason why the man chose me to meet you.''

''I guess they thought I'd be an easy touch.''

''Why would they?''

''My own life was falling apart. Pregnant. Alone. And everyone I worked with knew how I envied the undercover agents. I used to buy them beers just so they'd talk to me about their adventures. I think they made half of them up just to get me excited.''

''So if we buy that theory, the man would have to be someone you worked with that was already in league with Calderone.''

''Someone who knew the names of the files but didn't have access to them,'' she said. ''That's the catch.''

''Maybe it's someone who'd been fired or who just retired.''

Sarah sucked in a shaky breath. ''I know where you're going with that, Cody, but you're wrong. Grover Rucker is decent. Considerate.''

''And gone,'' Cody reminded her.

She shook her head, unwilling to believe such evil of the man she'd worked so closely with. ''If he planned to steal those files for Calderone,'' she argued, ''he would have waited until the code was put in place before he retired. Besides, he hated Calderone. I don't know how many times he said a man like that shouldn't live.''

''He was right about that. I've gone over and over this ever since we got back from the Smoking Barrel. I think if we work this just right, we might be the ones to get Calderone off the streets. Are you brave enough to try?''

"As long as you're beside me."

"All the way."

"Then tell me the plan. But first, I need you to do one thing."

"Name it."

"Kiss me, Cody. Long and wet and passionately."

"My pleasure."

Her lips melted into his, and her stomach twitched, a soft kick and then a harder one. Baby Joy knew something was up. Or maybe she was just giving her okay to the man her mom was falling in love with.

Chapter Thirteen

They sat in the swing on the front porch of the cabin, the phone Cody had borrowed from the Smoking Barrel clutched in his right hand, his left arm circling Sarah's shoulders.

Sarah turned to face him. "Are you sure you want to go through with this?"

"I'm sure I want to see this whole mess over and done with." And for her sake as well as his, Cody hoped this would finish it. He knew that even if the man agreed to his offer, he might be the one walking into the trap, but there was just a chance that he could pull it off. Then, with any luck, Sarah would likely draw a very light sentence or possibly a suspended one.

She could give her child all the love in the world. She'd adore it, watch over it, make it laugh and hold it to her breast when it cried. It would be one lucky baby. And Todd Benson was one terrific fool.

A mule deer stepped out of the brush, head high, watching them for a few seconds before jumping a ravine and heading back to a sheltered area beyond a scrub-covered hill.

"It seems so peaceful out here," Sarah said, lifting

her head to see the last quick movements of the deer. "You'd think it would be immune to crime."

"No area's immune to crime anymore." Cody nudged his Stetson back an inch or two on his head. "The Calderones of the world, the greedy, the controllers. They take what they want, any way they want."

"I know. The DPS doesn't seem to make a dent in the killings and the illegal drugs."

"That's because we play by the rules. Calderone makes his own rules."

Sarah moved her feet so that the swing swayed to an easy rhythm. "If we didn't play by the rules, we'd be just like him."

"You've been listening to too many politicians and do-gooders. Rules don't make us different from Calderone and other men like him. Decency makes us different. Even without rules, I'd never be able to do the things he's done or had someone else do for him. I couldn't kill a child or butcher a witness who was about to testify against me."

"But some lawmen could."

"They could and they do. The rules don't stop them. In the end it all comes down to what a man's made of. Whether or not he's decent."

She rested a hand on his thigh. "Spoken like a true lawman."

"An ex-lawman." He punched in the last phone number that had been left on his pager, rehearsing in his mind what he wanted to say. The phone only rang twice.

"Is that you, Cody?"

He recognized the voice at once. So much like the real Daniel Austin's that it made his stomach somersault. "Am I the only one who calls you?"

"You're the only one who has *this* number. Where in the devil have you been?"

"Around."

"I'd say. Your picture's been on every TV station in Texas. I'm sure it's also posted front and center in every hole-in-the-wall sheriff's office from Dallas to El Paso."

"I suppose you'd have liked it better if I'd just let the man at the fishing camp kill us. Then you wouldn't have to worry about where we were."

"I didn't have anything to do with that."

"Of course not. You're just trying to help the DPS."

"Damn it, Cody. You let Sarah Rand get to you. I can't believe it. I've risked my life trying to set this up and catch her in the act, and you let your hormones ruin the whole operation."

Cody felt his insides tighten, his muscles strain. He glanced at Sarah. The wind caught her hair, tossing wispy strands of it across her face. Her eyes were wide, greener than a spring pasture, her lips pink and full. He had fallen for her. There was no denying that. Fallen harder than he'd ever fallen for any woman in his life.

"Are you still there, Cody?"

"I'm here and I'm ready to bring you the disk."

"Will Miss Rand be with you?"

"She will."

"Good. Then I'll give you new directions. And I don't want there to be any screw-ups this time."

"No screw-ups, Daniel, but the terms have changed. Sarah and I will give you the disk in exchange for the million dollars you promised Sarah."

"What are you talking about? There is no money, Cody. I never planned to go through with the payoff.

You know that. I just wanted to catch her in the act of selling information to Calderone.''

''I think there is money. I think you lied. In fact I don't think you're Daniel Austin at all, but one of Calderone's flunkies.''

''You're way off base and making a big mistake.''

''Am I? I guess we'll find out.''

''If you mess this up, you're through with Texas Confidential forever. You're through with law enforcement period.''

''I am anyway. If this plays out the way I intend it to, I'll be through with work forever. We have the disk with the file you asked for. Do you want it or not?''

The silence seemed to stretch interminably. Now that Cody had come up with the idea, he wanted it to work so badly he could taste it. It would solve everything. He offered the man the same choice he'd offered Cody in the bar a few days ago. ''I'm waiting. All I need is a simple answer. Yes or no.''

He could hear the air release from the man's lungs. The sound of surrender.

''What are the terms?''

''One million dollars in cash and a private plane to fly us to the Cayman Islands.''

''I'll have to see if I can get it.''

''You can get it. Calderone will never even miss it. I'll call you tomorrow and tell you where to meet us. Oh, there is one other thing.''

''You're pushing your luck.''

''I want Calderone there. Sarah will only deliver the disk if she can put it in Calderone's hand.''

''This is the most absurd thing I've heard of. Tomaso Calderone does not dance to anyone's music but his own.''

"He will if he wants the disk. And I've seen what's on it, so I'm sure he does."

Cody hung up the phone without waiting for a reply. His hands were clammy, but for the first time since he'd met Sarah Rand he felt as if he had at least a small degree of control.

Sarah settled into the circle of his arm. "Did he agree to everything?"

"More or less."

"Do you think he really believes you'll turn it over to him?"

"He knows we're both in big trouble here. A million dollars and a flight to the Cayman Islands would go a long way toward solving our problems."

She tilted her face upward and locked her gaze with his. "You haven't really thought about taking the money and leaving the country, have you?"

He trailed a finger from her forehead to her mouth and then outlined the softness of her lips. "Sure. But what would a cowboy do in the Cayman Islands?"

"You don't fool me for a second, Cody Gannon. You could never sell out to the enemy. A man is what he is, and you're the most decent, honest man I've ever met."

"Think your mom would be impressed?"

"She'd love you." Stretching, she touched her lips to his. "What's not to love?"

Love. The word made him uneasy. It made him think of commitment and marriage and family. Come to think of it, all those words made him uncomfortable. They carried bad connotations. The legacy of Frank Gannon and Mitchell Forbes.

Sarah ran her hand along his leg. He could feel the heat right through the denim. Her fingers slid to his inner thigh, stroking until she was touching parts of him that made him crazy for more. He was sure she knew what she was doing to him.

He caught her hand in his. "Don't tell me danger turns you on?"

"It always has. Me, Sarah Rand, just about to be front and center in a plot to bring down the mighty Tomaso Calderone."

"There will be risks. Even if I can talk the other Confidential agents into getting involved, nothing is guaranteed."

"We'll win, Cody. I know we will. I feel it, and my mother always said that when your heart is light, your dreams will come true." She feathered his lips with kisses. "Make love to me, Cody."

"Out here?"

"Why not? There's a shady patch of grass just to the left of that big rock and there's a blanket on the seat of that old rocker in the living room."

"The ground's hard and the blanket will make us itch."

"I'll scratch you where it itches."

"In that case, I'll be right back with the most abrasive blanket I can find."

SARAH LAY on her back and watched Cody take off his boots and unzip his jeans. "I like to watch you undress."

"It's usually the man who says that."

"Not anymore. Modern women say what they're thinking, and I'm thinking that I love to watch you step out of your jeans. Your knees are a little knobby, but your thighs are to die for."

The jeans slipped from his fingers and he dropped down beside her. "I like all of you," he said.

"That's too broad a statement. What do you like best about me?"

"Your gorgeous eyes." He kissed the tip of her forehead and both of her eyelids. "The way your hair catches the sunlight and seems to be on fire." He brushed a lock behind her ear and kissed her earlobe. "Your smile."

This time he kissed her lips, soft for a second and then so intense she lost herself in him. She'd wanted the lovemaking to be slow this time, but once they started, she couldn't hold back. His mouth roamed her body while his fingers loosened the buttons on her blouse. In seconds she was naked and going crazy with desire. And still Cody primed her, kissing her neck, her breasts, the swell of her stomach. She was familiar with all the usual spots a man touched to turn a woman on, but Cody found new places that made her body scream to be fulfilled.

"I love how you love me, Cody. This is what you think it will be like, but it never is, the way it is in movies and novels."

He laughed and rolled her over on top of him. She looked into his eyes. "Did I say something funny?"

"No, you just amaze me. Even when you're making love, you talk."

"Doesn't everybody?"

"You're asking a man who can go all day without saying a dozen words. But talk all you want. Just as long as you still find time to kiss me."

So she did. All over, until he writhed in sweet agony. Then she guided him inside her. She didn't talk then, couldn't even think. All she could do was feel. Like

Christmas and New Year's and the Fourth of July all rolled into one. He climaxed quickly, and she felt the energy burst from his body and enter hers. Perfect. Glorious. Cody.

Finally, passion spent, she lay beside him. Somewhere Tomaso Calderone was preparing to meet them. A world of danger, and yet life had never felt so right. It had never even come close.

CODY WALKED OUT the back door and down the steps. The wind had picked up, blowing in from the north again. Some of the natives were predicting an extra cold winter this year. They might be right. Not that he'd be here to enjoy it.

At the rate things were going, he might be in jail. He'd been certain Calderone would jump on his offer to sell him the disk, but two days had passed since he'd offered the deal and no one had paged him with the go-ahead.

Under the circumstances, he was glad he hadn't mentioned this to Rafe yet. Not that Rafe would have said so, but he could imagine what he'd be thinking. Another farfetched idea by the outsider. The man who'd been handed a place on the Texas Confidential team when everyone else had to earn theirs.

No wonder they'd joked that he had no specialty. No experience. No training. No skills. They were right. So why had he ever imagined he could lure Calderone into a trap when better men had tried it and ended up dead?

That's why when it came right down to the act, he wasn't taking Sarah with him, though he wasn't going to get into that with her until he had to.

He'd had to promise she'd be there to lure Calderone, but he'd never take chances with her life. It would be him and hopefully the rest of Texas Confidential, out of sight, but available for backup. He had the equipment he'd taken from the Smoking Barrel all ready to go. He'd be wired so that he could capture the conversation on tape. And he'd be armed.

But would he be a match for Calderone?

A door slammed shut behind him. Sarah must have decided to join him. She was probably as nervous as he was, though you'd never know it. She'd sung in the shower this morning, danced all around him while he'd tried to scramble eggs, kissed him senseless while he'd tried to help her with the dishes.

He was glad for her upbeat mood. What he wasn't glad of was that she'd started talking as if they were a thing. Not a temporary, get-out-of-this-alive thing, but a *real* thing. Showed how little she knew about him.

Sarah walked up behind him and slid her arms about his waist. "Calderone will call today, Cody. I have a feeling about it."

"Unless he's figured out the code has already been changed."

"Even if he has, you shouldn't blame yourself. You've done everything a man can do, including save my life at least a couple of times. You're the bravest and smartest agent I've ever met."

"I'm sure Mitchell Forbes would be able to point out a few mistakes I've made."

She dropped her hands from his waist and walked around to stand in front of him. "What is it with you and Mitchell Forbes? I always get the feeling there's some kind of love-hate struggle going on between the two of you."

"You've never seen us together."

"I don't have to. I hear what you say and the way

you look when you talk about him. I saw your reaction when you talked about him with Penny the other night.''

As usual Sarah was right on target. His first impulse was to lie, but she'd see right through it. And yet, he didn't want to tell her the truth. He'd never said it out loud to anyone, and having never said that Mitchell was his real father made it seem less true.

He looked up and tracked a bird that flew just above an outcropping of rock. ''We may need the fireplace again tonight. If we're still here.''

''No fair changing the subject.'' She took his hands in hers. ''Sometimes it helps to talk.''

''This isn't one of those times.'' But he knew she wouldn't give up and go away. That was his style, not hers. But maybe she needed to hear the truth about who he really was. Then she'd realize he was not the man to play daddy to her baby.

The wind gusted, tossing dust into the air. He rubbed the grit from his eyes and walked over to a large rock. Propping his backside against it, he waited for Sarah to follow.

She wasted no time in doing it. ''Did Mitchell call when you saved the little girl and foiled the bank robbery attempt or did he just show up at your door?''

''He called, said he had a proposition for me, one I couldn't afford to pass up. He had me meet him here at the hunting cabin.''

''Did you rush right over?''

''Nope. I'd already paid my entry fee in the next day's competition at the rodeo. I took first place, collected my winnings and drove out here, thinking all the time I was probably wasting my time.''

''But you joined up with Texas Confidential?''

"Naive as I was, I took Mitchell at his word. Believed he was impressed with my heroic deeds. I realized soon enough that no one at the Smoking Barrel was half as impressed as the folks at the newspaper and television stations had been. They needed a story, but it was no big deal."

"You saved a life, Cody. I'm sure it was a big deal to the little girl and to her mother."

"I did what anyone would have done, given the chance."

"A bank full of people had the same chance you did. They did nothing."

"It still didn't make me agent material."

"Mitchell must have thought that it did."

"No, he thought he'd absolve a lifetime of guilt with one act."

"Why would he be guilty?"

"He supplied the sperm for my birth." There, he'd said it.

Sarah's eyebrows drew together. "You mean, he was a donor?"

"You might say that. He slept with my mother. She got pregnant with me. End of story."

She frowned. "Another Todd. But everyone talks about Mitchell Forbes like he's such a hero. A man of honor."

"Yeah, well he left my mom on her own. She was probably like you, looking for someone to step in and be the man Mitchell wasn't."

"Did she marry someone else?"

"Frank Gannon. I thought he was my father for all those years. I thought his blood ran through me. Half the time I thought I hated my mom for doing that to me, and all the time I hated Frank Gannon for making my mother's life and mine a living hell.''

''Why? What was wrong with him?''

''He drank too much. When he did, he became violent. I hated him for every bruise he put on my mother's body. For every drop of blood she lost because he'd knocked her into a wall or onto the hard kitchen floor.''

''Did he hurt you as well?''

''Sometimes. She always put herself between the two of us. She took blows for me and I couldn't do a thing about it. That made it even worse.''

''You were just a child, Cody. You couldn't stop a grown man.''

''I know that now, but just knowing it doesn't erase the past.'' Now that Cody had started talking, he couldn't stop. He'd kept it all inside for so many years. Worn his tough exterior like some kind of shield.

''As a kid I cried myself to sleep on those horrible nights and wished that Frank Gannon would die, prayed that I'd find out that he was not my dad. And all the time, he wasn't. Mitchell Forbes was. Powerful rancher. Tough-as-nails lawman. Never once did he come and see if me and my mom were all right.''

Sarah wrapped her fingers around his forearm. ''Maybe he did, Cody. Maybe he did, but your mother didn't tell you.''

''He didn't show up when she died. I went through that alone and then I went back to that house and slept with the memories of what she'd gone through.''

''When did you find out he was your father?''

''A week ago.''

''No wonder you still feel the pain so intensely. He must have told you after he had the heart attack. But at least he wants to make peace with you, share some kind of bond before it's too late.''

''He never told me. I overheard it. But it doesn't matter now. It's all over. I was never a real Confidential agent, anyway. Everyone knew that except me. That's what hurts most of all. To know that I preened around there, thinking I was finally somebody. Only I never really was. The job was just a token offering for the sins of my father.''

''I think you should call him, Cody. I know how you feel, but he may die in that surgery. Call him and make peace before it's too late.''

He turned and stepped away from her. ''It's already too late, Sarah. About thirty years too late.'' He stared out at the rocks and craggy mountains but didn't really see them. The images in his mind were too compelling. The sights and sounds of a bloody past.

''I need to go inside, Cody.''

Something in Sarah's voice triggered an alarm. He spun around. She was leaning against the rock. Her hands were cupped under her stomach and he could read the fear in her eyes.

''Is it the baby?''

''I think something's wrong. I'm having pains in my abdomen and lower back.''

His blood ran cold. ''Not contractions?''

''I'm not sure. But it doesn't feel right. Help me inside. I need to lie down.''

''It's my fault. I shouldn't have brought you out here to this wilderness. I should have just taken you to the police and let them handle this or else let you keep running when you got away from me at the airport.''

''If you'd taken me to the police I'd be in jail with an open-and-shut case against me. If you'd left me alone, I'd be dead. Now don't argue with me. Just help me back to the house. I will not lose this baby."

He lifted her in his arms and carried her down the rocky slope toward the cabin. He'd looked killers in the face and never been as scared as he was this minute.

TOMASO CALDERONE stepped out of the private jet that had just landed on American soil. He dusted his hands and waited for Marcus Slade. The man's thin lips twitched and his bald head looked like a melon ripening in the sun. Calderone was amazed, as always, at how nondescript he looked when he was not in disguise.

"Just how far are we from this mountain cabin where our little pregnant princess is hiding?" he asked, when Marcus reached his side.

"About fifty miles." Marcus fingered the brim of the hat he was holding. "There is an incredible shortage of landing strips in this part of Texas."

"But you are sure she is there?"

"She's there. She and Cody Gannon."

"Just the two of them, and no one else?"

"No one else." Marcus rubbed his bald head, then plopped his hat over the speckled flesh. "The cowboy took her there to protect her. Can you imagine a man who thinks he can protect a woman who has reneged on a deal with Tomaso Calderone?"

"I can imagine it well, especially after the way your two buffoons botched up the mission."

"They were not *my* buffoons. They work for you, sir."

"A mistake I plan to remedy. Nonetheless, you were in charge of getting that file. Instead you made front-page news all over Texas with your blunders. And that makes me very unhappy." Calderone could see both hatred and fear reflected in Slade's beady eyes. As it should be. A man couldn't rule if his men didn't fear and respect him.

"Get the car, Slade. I want you and Berto to ride with me. The others can follow us. Do you have the guns?"

"Exactly as you asked. They won't have a chance against our weapons. They'll be as helpless as clay pigeons on a fence post."

"They'll die, but unless I have those files in my hands today, they will not be the only ones who go down. You do comprehend what I'm saying?"

Sweat beaded on his horrid brow. "*Si*. I understand completely."

Chapter Fourteen

Cody settled Sarah in her bed and then went back to the den in search of the phone. His mind flew into a panic. He couldn't think straight, couldn't remember where he'd left it. He always hated that about portable phones. The worse you needed them the harder they were to locate.

He uttered a few curses that didn't help at all, irritated with himself. He was known for keeping a cool head when it counted most. Obviously that didn't apply to handling pregnant women.

"Cody."

Sarah's call stopped him in his tracks. He raced to the bedroom door to see what new emergency had developed.

Both hands were on her belly, but she managed a strained smile. "The phone's in the kitchen."

"Right." He raced to the kitchen, found the phone and punched in the number for the Smoking Barrel while he headed back to the bedroom. His breath went on hold as the third ring started. Finally it was Rosa who picked up.

"*Alo?*"

"Rosa, this is Cody. I need Penny. *Es urgente.*"

"She's out on her horse. I page her?"

"Yes. *Dile que* Sarah…" His Spanish failed him. He'd just have to make Rosa understand. "Sarah, the woman I was with the other night is having some pain."

"*Mucho?* A lot?"

"*Si.*" Cody dropped to the side of the bed next to Sarah. "She's in bed."

Sarah grabbed the phone from his hand. "I'm scared. It hurts. No, not *mucho* now."

Cody couldn't hear Rosa's end of the conversation, but whatever she was saying, it seemed to calm Sarah. He could use a little of that talk himself.

"*Si,* Rosa. I'll go and see Penny's doctor." She handed the phone back to Cody.

Rosa started one of her lectures, half in English, half in Spanish. He had trouble following her, but the gist of the message was that he should call a doctor and he should call Mitchell Forbes.

Call Mitchell. That was the answer for everything around the Smoking Barrel. He used to think that way himself.

"You listen to Rosa, Cody?"

"I am. Thanks, Rosa. I still need you to page Penny for me. Is Rafe around?"

"No. All the *hombres* leave. All excited. They do something fun, I think."

"What about Kendra or Catherine? Are they there?"

"All ladies go to hospital to see Mitchell."

So Mitchell was back in bed where he was supposed to be. He wondered if it was by choice or if he'd collapsed in some DPS office. But he couldn't worry about that now. "Just have Penny call me. She has the number."

He broke the connection. All the Confidential agents had left together and excited enough that Rosa took notice. The something big Penny had talked about the other night must be going down. Which meant if Calderone called now, Cody would have no backup. He'd still go through with it, though. He might never have a chance like this again.

But first he had to take care of Sarah. He splayed his hand across her belly. "Are you still having the shooting pains?"

"They've settled into more of a dull ache in my lower back. I think it may have been a panic attack."

"You told Rosa you'd see a doctor."

"I will. Get the name of Penny's doctor when she calls. I'll see him."

He stroked her belly, softly, like he might do a kitten, as always awed by the fact that life grew inside Sarah. "Looks like little Joy is trying to tell you to slow down. You've had a rough week."

She laid her hand on top of his. "It's been the most exciting week of my life."

"Running from the law and the lawless?"

"Living on the edge. Leaving my humdrum life for something daring. Knowing that we have a chance to bring Calderone down." She paused then trailed the fingers of her right hand down the back of his neck. "Meeting you. My first real cowboy."

"So many cowboys. So little time," he teased, quoting the message on her infamous tote bag.

"Too little time. Joy and I would settle for one cowboy, as long as it's you. Only if you don't promise to stay calmer than you did a minute ago, we're not going to invite you to the hospital for the crowning moment of her birth."

Cody felt the tightening again, the suffocating sensation that seemed to cut off his breath. Sarah pictured him at the birth of her baby. Pictured him in her life. He couldn't. Couldn't see himself anywhere people counted on him day in and day out. He'd probably have wound up in jail long ago if Mitchell hadn't lurked around like some freaky fairy godmother, yanking him out of trouble. He stared out the window, mainly because he couldn't look Sarah in the eye.

"You don't have to climb back into your shell, Cody. I didn't ask you to marry me. I don't need a husband. I don't need anyone. I can take care of myself. I have an apartment. This is all going to work out. The DPS may even call me and want me back. I'll be just fine. My mother will…" Her voice broke. "I talk too much."

Cody turned around. Her hands were clasped over her stomach. Her eyes were moist. "You don't talk too much. You don't do anything too much. You'll be a perfect mother and a perfect wife."

"Just not for you."

He swallowed hard. He'd do anything not to upset her. Even lie to her if he thought she wouldn't see right through him. "It's not you, Sarah." He tried to think of something that would lighten the moment. "It's my aura," he said.

"The Texas dust?"

"No, you called it from the first. It's dark."

"I was seeing it in the wrong light."

"You were right on target. I'm nothing but trouble. I don't even have a job."

"You'll find another one or else you'll go back to Texas Confidential."

"There's no longer a place for me there."

"Then there'll be a place for you somewhere else in the DPS. You're too good at what you do. I should know."

"I'm fast on the trigger. Never miss a target. The man of the hour. Sometimes even the man of the week. But never the man of a lifetime."

"How do you know if you never give yourself a chance?"

"I know because I'm Frank Gannon's boy."

"Frank Gannon was a monster, and his blood does not run through your veins."

"No, but his influence does. I'm not husband material. Not father material either. I'm not proud of the fact. But wanting it to be different won't change it."

"I'd take a chance on you any day of the week."

"But I can't let you."

She met his gaze and didn't look away. "I just want to know one thing, and I expect you to be honest with me."

"If I can."

"Do you have feelings for me? I don't mean love necessarily. It might be too soon for you to know that. I just want to know if making love with me meant anything to you, because it sure did to me."

"It meant something." He walked to the door, afraid to stay. Afraid he'd break down and make promises he'd never be able to keep. But he stopped. He hadn't been completely honest and he owed her that. "It meant everything."

CODY WENT to the kitchen and started a fresh pot of coffee. He paced the floor while it brewed, listening for any sound from the bedroom where Sarah was resting. Penny hadn't called back yet. He needed her help with this, needed her vehicle as well. But if the sharp pains started again, he wasn't going to wait around. They were going to the hospital and take their chances that they wouldn't be picked up by state troopers before they made it.

The coffee finished brewing. He poured himself a cup and went down the hall to check on his patient. She was on her side, her knees pulled up, her hair fanning out over the pillow. Fast asleep.

Sweet, sexy, pregnant Sarah. That's the way he'd always see her in his mind. Such a nice image to go with the million dreadful ones that lived there.

The phone rang. He ran to answer it, hoping it wouldn't wake Sarah. Before he finished the hello, Penny hit him with questions.

"Is Sarah all right? Have you called a doctor?"

"I think the pain has eased. She's asleep, and we haven't talked to a doctor. She wanted you to recommend one."

"I can give you the name and phone number of my gynecologist or I can go with you to see him if you like. I doubt he'd recognize Sarah from the pictures in the paper unless he saw the two of you together. She's much cuter than that grainy shot. And he wouldn't have reason to suspect anything if I just said she was a friend visiting from out of town."

Penny, as always, had come through in a clutch. "I appreciate your offer, and Sarah definitely will. Having this baby means everything to her."

"I'm sure. Do you want to tell me where you are or should I meet you somewhere?"

"It would be best if you meet us. We'll need to go in your car. I don't want to drive mine into town, not with the description of it riding with every lawman on the road.''

''I was going to suggest that. Where shall we meet?''

''How about where the dirt road crosses Garvey Creek to get to Jake's cabin.''

''How long will it take you to get there?''

Cody hesitated for a second. Giving her a time was the same as giving her a distance. From there, it wouldn't be too difficult to figure out where he and Sarah were staying. Only it probably didn't matter any longer. One way or another this would all be over soon.

''We'll meet you in forty-five minutes.''

''I'll be there. And one more thing. Don't drive like a maniac. Those roads around Jake's place have more ruts than a soybean field. And a bumpy road is the last thing Sarah needs.''

PENNY DIDN'T take time to change. In this part of the country, jeans and a western shirt were appropriate for every social and business event. Stopping by the kitchen, she told Rosa she was going out. A whiff of freshly-baked cookies caught her attention and she grabbed several from the plate on the counter.

''Oatmeal raisin. My favorite.''

''Take more. For Cody and the pregnant lady.''

''What makes you think I'm going to see Cody?''

''I not so good at English, but my eyes *mucho* good. I know.''

''Well, keep all this stuff you *see* under your sunbonnet.'' Penny took a few extra cookies and wrapped them in a napkin. Snagging her jacket from the hook by the door and the hat from the chair where she'd tossed it, she headed out to meet Cody.

She'd be in the car with him and Sarah. Maybe this

time she could learn a little more about what was going on between them. She still wouldn't be a bit surprised if all this turned out to be part of some undercover scheme Mitchell and the DPS had cooked up. If it was, they had certainly taken it to the limits.

She jumped behind the wheel of her Jeep Cherokee. Yanking the gearshift into reverse, she backed up and turned around, kicking up choking clouds of dust as she did.

Cody had said that Sarah was sleeping, so she was probably in no immediate danger of losing the baby. But adrenaline pumped into Penny's system, feeding an urgency she couldn't explain. It had been there even before she'd gotten the SOS from Cody.

The imminence of danger. It rode with her today. Maybe she'd caught the anxiety from the Confidential agents that morning. Maybe it was knowing that Mitchell was growing weaker instead of stronger, and pushing himself beyond human limits.

She hoped Cody and Sarah were part of an undercover scheme. If not, she would be guilty of aiding and abetting fugitives from justice. But, covert operation or not, Cody was no criminal and he was nobody's fool. If he was convinced that the woman he was protecting was innocent, then Penny would have to act on that same assumption. She pressed her foot down harder on the accelerator. She wasn't pregnant. She could take the bumpy ride.

She turned off one dirt road and onto another. This one ran past the south pasture and around the horse grazing area. If she could fly like the crow, this would be a short trip, but she had to follow the road or get stopped by gulches and ravines created by runoff from the Davis mountains.

She fingered the dial of the radio and found a distant station that played country music with static for background. That was the best she could get this far from the station, but it took the edge off the loneliness that always invaded her when she visited this part of the ranch. The house had disappeared from sight long ago. It was only her, coyotes and a few foxes, and always the snakes and lizards that slithered through the grass. And, of course, grazing cattle and majestic horses.

Usually she had her phone with her when she was out this far, but hers had come up missing the night Cody had visited the Smoking Barrel. No secret to her what had happened to it.

The road turned south, toward Garvey Creek. She hated the narrow bridge that crossed it. One day, she was going to misjudge the width by an inch and go crashing over the side and into the running water. Only cowboys would build a bridge without side rails. They never expected to make mistakes.

She slowed as another vehicle came into view. Pulled off the road on her left and about a hundred yards in front of her. A cattle hauler.

Odd. She was chief paper shuffler in matters of the ranch and she didn't recall that anyone was supposed to be hauling cattle away this week.

She slowed to a crawl as she came up even with the truck. It was loaded with restless, mooing critters. No driver. So where was he? And who was he?

She pulled over and stopped. Two men were standing down by the creek, tossing rocks at something in the water. Neither turned. Apparently they hadn't heard her drive up. One was long and lanky, not much muscle. The other short and pudgy with a wide neck and bowed legs. They both wore black hats, like stereotypical bad guys in a western movie.

Bad guys. Ohmigod! These were the rustlers they'd been trying to catch for months. Only this time they'd really gotten brazen. They'd driven their ugly cattle hauler right onto the ranch and loaded the cattle on the spot.

Her mind went a thousand ways at once. Call for help. No phone.

You wanted more responsibility, Penny Archer. You got it. You wanted to learn to handle a gun. You did.

It was fate. Opening her glove compartment, she reached inside and pulled out her pistol.

Easing the door open, she stepped out. A few steps. *Make sure you're in shooting range. Never take chances.* Rafe's warnings hammered in her brain as she ducked out of sight and crept toward the creek. Closer and closer.

She took a deep breath, aimed her pistol and stepped into the open. "Stick your hands in the air and turn around real slow. And don't even think about going for your gun." The fat man hesitated. She fired just over his head. "Not that slow."

She had their attention now. And the adrenaline was flowing like wine. She'd always thought she was missing out on something great by not getting into the real action. Now she knew it.

"I'M FEELING much better now, Cody. I think we could postpone this trip to the doctor."

"What do you have against doctor's offices?"

"Nothing. It's jails I have an aversion to."

Cody walked to the kitchen to pull down the windows he'd raised earlier. The wind was kicking up again, and there were clouds building up in the west. "Penny thinks we can pull this off, that the doctor won't recognize you as the woman from the fishing camp."

"Penny won't be the one going to jail if he does."

"You can get out on bail."

"Yeah, all my secretary friends have hundreds of thousands of dollars to put up for my release." She followed him into the kitchen. "It's not just the chance of being arrested. I want us to nail Calderone. It's the only way I'll ever prove my story. He has millions of dollars to buy his witnesses. I can't even afford to take mine to dinner."

"I haven't given up on that."

"But he should have paged you by now. Are you sure that thing is working? Maybe the batteries ran down."

"I've checked it a dozen times today. Now get your coat. You may need it by the time we get back to the cabin."

"It's by the door. I'll get it and meet you at the truck."

Cody made a quick pass down the hall, checking windows, turning off the lights, just in case they didn't make it back. He'd tried to sound positive for Sarah's benefit, but he knew it was only a matter of time before they were taken into custody. He could take her and run, leave Texas, hide out like common criminals, but that had never been his intention.

All he'd wanted to do was protect her until he could find out who wanted her dead and why a man who called himself Daniel Austin had dragged them into the scheme. But it was more than responsibility that was bonding him to her now. It was attraction so strong he couldn't think rationally anymore, not where she was concerned. An attraction that had nowhere to go.

SARAH TOOK the steps easy, not wanting to do anything to start the pains shooting through her lower back again. But she'd felt a solid kick a few minutes ago. Little Joy was still strong and cradled inside her.

She walked toward the truck. A strong hand on her arm stopped her. "So we finally meet, Miss Rand."

Panic gripped her, stealing her breath and her voice. She stared at the man. His eyes were dark, cold, intimidating. An expensive suit jacket fit perfectly over his broad shoulders. A huge diamond glistened on his finger.

"Who are you?"

"Don't you know? You invited me to come calling."

Her stomach turned inside out. "Calderone."

Chapter Fifteen

Sarah's heart turned inside out. "Tomaso Calderone."

"In the flesh," Calderone answered, his diction perfect, his tone sophisticated. He touched the short barrel of a pistol to her temple. "You should feel honored. I don't travel to the barren ranges of west Texas for just anyone. I found your invitation intriguing."

"How did you find us?"

"You made it easy. Our friend Marcus followed you from the Smoking Barrel when you visited the other night."

"You were supposed to page us." Stupid remark, but her mind had frozen in some time warp of cold fear. She had to warn Cody. But how? If she called him, he'd think she was in pain again and come running.

She turned at the sound of shuffling feet in the brush to her left. Two more men stood waiting, both holding guns. She had to do something and do it fast before Cody walked out the door and into the trap.

"I'm glad you decided to come," she whispered. "I'll go into the house and get the diskette so that we can make the exchange."

Calderone's laugh filled the air around them, sent

fear jabbing into her chest. Memories raced through her mind. Bloody body parts stuffed into a cardboard box.

"There's been a little change in plans, Miss Rand."

"You're going to kill me, aren't you?"

"Me? Kill a pretty thing like you? Why would I do such a heartless thing? You'll make a nice addition to my harem."

"Then shoot me now. I'd sooner be dead than share a bed with you."

"You'll change your mind. They always do. Power is the most seductive force in the world."

He let go of her arm and trailed one smooth finger down her cheek. Her flesh crawled, and she tried to shrink away from his touch. He smiled, clearly enjoying her reaction. Then, in a swift, powerful movement, he wrapped his arm about her waist pulling her to him like a shield.

"Call our little Texas Confidential buddy. It's time for him to get in on the fun."

"It's a trap…"

Calderone interrupted her yell with the palm of his hand. He covered her nose as well, stopping the flow of oxygen while she tried to push him away. The world started to fade around her. Shades of gray, so blurry she could barely make out Cody's frame as he stepped out the front door of the cabin and onto the porch.

Calderone removed his hand from her face and she gasped, her body shaking as air penetrated to her lungs. The images grew clearer. Cody was on the porch, holding up the disk in his left hand, a pistol in his right.

"I have what you want Calderone. Let the lady go, and it's yours."

"You've been a Confidential agent too long to think I can be threatened by some two-bit cowboy lawman,

Cody Gannon. Look around you. You're surrounded. I call *all* the shots.''

She watched as Cody visually assessed the situation, his gaze moving from her and Calderone to the two men standing to his left and then back to her. Three guns were pointed at him. Three to his one.

She had to do something, but Calderone's powerful arm was locked around her, holding her close. Nauseous and dizzy from the temporary lack of oxygen, she had to force herself to concentrate.

"Let Sarah go. Let her walk into the house unhurt or I'll blow this disk into a million pieces."

"If you destroy the disk, you'll be coyote bait, Cody. And Sarah here will go back to Mexico with me to feed my cravings." He laughed again and she felt the rumble of his body pressing into hers, grew sick from the peppery smell of his breath and the repugnant odor of the sweet cologne on his sweaty body.

"Lay the disk on the porch railing, Cody, and step away."

"And then you'd get it all. Sarah for your pleasures, the DPS classified code to make it even easier for you to ply your stinking drug trade without getting apprehended, and my dead body to send to my friends."

"You have no friends. That's why you played along with us to start with. You were a prime candidate to meet Sarah. That way if it was a trap, it would be you who was caught in it, you who was imprisoned for the offense. Especially when your only alibi was that a dead man had enlisted your help."

"I have no friends. But I have the disk. If you want it, you'll play my way."

Calderone turned to his men. "If he destroys the disk, shoot to kill."

"And if I don't destroy it, they'll still shoot to kill."

"So what do you plan to do?"

"Take out at least one of you before I go. Let's see. Who would you choose if you were me? One of your two *nothing* guys. Or the big man himself?"

"If you kill me, the bullet will have to go through Sarah first."

"Better dead than with your filthy hands all over her body. What do you say, Sarah? Shall I kill him?"

"Pull the trigger, Cody." She, Cody and the baby. She'd dreamed of them living together as a family. Now they'd die together. And all because she'd made a horrible mistake, thought that for once in her life she could do something important, that Sarah Rand could make a difference. Now she finally would.

"Pull the trigger and blow this rotten, murderous sicko away."

Something moved in the bushes next to the two men. The bald man moved first, jumped into the air, and screamed, "Snake!" The sound of gunfire exploded in Sarah's head. Over and over and over. The arm that had held her erect dropped from around her and she slumped to the ground. Blood was everywhere. On her shirt, rolling down her arms, dripping onto her slacks.

She looked up. Cody was standing over her. She wasn't sure if she was dead or alive, but she knew what she felt and she wasn't afraid anymore. "I love you, Cody. I love you."

"I love you, too, Sarah."

She smiled. If she was dead, heaven was a nice place to be.

CODY KICKED Calderone's gun, sending it careening end over end across the hard earth. The man was bleeding, seriously wounded, but not dead. Still, he wouldn't be causing anyone any trouble for awhile. One of his *hombres* had taken a bullet to the brain. The other had set off through the brush, into no-man's land. Cody had let him go while he rushed to Sarah.

He helped her to a sitting position. "I tend to keep asking the same question, but are you all right?"

"I'm not sure. Is this my blood?"

"Now that hurts my feelings. Shooting is my area of expertise, and I never miss my target."

"Cocky cowboy, aren't you?"

"I am now. A minute ago I was shaking in my boots."

The whir of helicopter blades invaded the victory party. His hand flew to his gun. He should have known this was too good to last.

Sarah groaned. "Not more of Calderone's men?"

He was about to order her to take cover in the brush when the chopper circled into view. "What do you know?" he said, helping her to her feet. "Texas Confidential is coming in. Only this time the outsider got here first. You gotta love this."

SARAH AND CODY sat in the small office while Dr. Donnelly scribbled something on a prescription pad. The frown on his face did not boost Sarah's level of confidence. The examination had been lengthy and punctuated by frequent "hmm's" and "uh-huh's" by the doctor.

She'd stood the quiet as long as she could stand it. "Look, doc, just give me the facts. Is the baby all right? I mean, a little back pain—even a lot of back pain— that's to be expected. Isn't it? I've taken my vitamins every day, and I haven't lifted anything heavy, well not much anyway. I eat well, and I'm hardly ever sick to my stomach, unless I eat enchiladas, of course. But the baby is kicking and everything, and..."

She stopped for breath. She was doing it again, rambling on and on. She wrung her hands together and sucked in a major gulp of air. "The baby has to be all right. I don't even care if it's a boy or a girl anymore. I just want it to be healthy."

The doctor cleared his throat. "The baby's fine, Miss Rand. A strong heartbeat, the appropriate size for your due date, and strong legs. I felt it kick myself. And, as far as I can tell without waiting for results of the blood tests and urinalysis, you're fine, too. Take a few days off and get some rest. After that, you might think about adding some excitement to your life. Nothing strenuous, just something to get your mind off the baby."

She gulped. "You want me to add excitement to my life?"

"I'd suggest it."

She looked at him and then at Cody and then started to giggle. The hysterical kind. The type that made her sides hurt and tears roll down her cheeks.

Cody tugged her to a standing position and wrapped his hand around her waist.

"She's a very emotional young woman," the doctor said, staring at her over his wire-rimmed spectacles.

"Extremely," Cody agreed. "I'll get her out of here."

By the time they hit the sidewalk in front of his office, they were both roaring.

"The rest of the gang is meeting at a local bar for drinks," he said when he managed to control his laughter. "Care to join them? You can order fruit juice."

"Why not? I need a little excitement in my life."

CODY PUSHED through the door at Vaqueros. He spotted Rafe and the rest of the group at a table in the back of the nearly deserted bar. Even at a time like this, they had to keep up their front. Just the hands from the Smoking Barrel out for a little fun.

He pulled out the chair next to Penny's and held it while Sarah slid into it.

"What's the report from the doctor's office?" Penny asked, scooting her chair over to give Sarah and Cody a little more room. "It must be good if you're here celebrating with this group."

"The baby's fine, but the doc thinks I need more excitement in my life."

"Oh, yeah. If the man only knew." She picked up a spoon and tapped it against her drink glass to get the others' attention. "The doctor says Sarah's life is too boring. Anyone know an activity that can beat what she went through today?"

"I could let her ride that bull that's been giving me fits," Brady said, when the laughter died down enough to talk. "But that would be a walk in the park compared to the activities Cody picks out for her."

Rafe walked over and put a hand on her right shoulder. "Forget the doc. What does he know? Besides, it's party time."

Everyone echoed their agreement. Jake raised his glass in a salute. "To the man who single-handedly brought down the powerful Tomaso Calderone." He kept his voice low enough that the cowboys at the bar wouldn't hear his toast over the jukebox, but the excitement came through loud and clear.

The hoopla embarrassed Cody, but pleased him, too. He wasn't even a Texas Confidential agent anymore, yet he'd never felt more a part of the team. He'd felt the bond at the cabin when they'd arrived just in time to take the injured Calderone to the hospital. But they'd listened to the details of the shooting quietly then, the way men did when their emotions were too raw or the event too big.

"Let's not forget Sarah," Cody said, anxious not only to take some of the attention off of himself but to give her the credit she deserved. "The woman behind the man."

"From what I heard she was in front of the man about half the time," Rafe joked. "We're signing her on. She can pose as a pregnant secret agent. I hear they're very effective."

"And then there's our own Penny, the gunslinger," Jake said. "She's added capturing cattle rustlers to her resume. Next thing we know she'll be after our jobs."

"I already am," she said, clapping him on the back.

Someone stuck a beer in Cody's hand. He downed half of it in a single gulp. That's when he spied the man at the end of the table. Sun-bleached hair, new wrinkles around his eyes, thinner than Cody remembered him. He stared for a few minutes, then moved down to take a seat next to him.

"Daniel Austin. I thought you were a dead man."

"I almost was. I was Calderone's prisoner for several weeks. When I escaped, the DPS decided to let me play dead a little longer. I was assigned to find the man responsible for leaking DPS secrets to Calderone."

Cody shook his head. "Don't tell me you're actually the man who approached me in that bar last week."

"Afraid not. That was Marcus Slade, my protégé in Calderone's camp, though I didn't mean for him to learn all my tricks. He was also the man who got away this afternoon. Fortunately we tracked him down easily enough. He's in the jail now, singing like a nightingale, and hoping it will buy him a little leniency from the judge. If Calderone lives, we'll have enough to put him away for a half dozen lifetimes.''

"Sarah copied the file containing the code, Daniel, but she thought she was helping you. And she wasn't responsible for the earlier leaks.''

"We know. Her ex-boss was. When we went to question Grover Rucker this week about Sarah, we found that he'd taken all his savings from the bank, bought a one-way ticket to Switzerland and was about to ride away into the sunset.''

"Did you stop him?''

"We did, and that's when he gave us a fascinating story about how he suspected Sarah was the leak and was determined to stop her. He claimed he'd set it up for her to steal the files and sell them to Calderone. And he had. Only it wasn't to trap her, but to buy time for himself and to hopefully appease Calderone enough that he wouldn't kill him the way he did everyone else when they were no longer any use to him.''

"So Rucker was the secret agent I heard about.''

"That was his story.''

"That explains why Sarah was chosen for the operation. Rucker knew how much she hated Calderone.'' Cody took another swig of his beer. "But why go to all that trouble? If he was the leak, why did he retire before he could copy the code himself?''

"He had no choice. Some discrepancies were discovered in his record keeping, and he was told to retire or be fired. I'm sure that's why Rucker gave Calderone the name of the file containing the code. Buying time until he could get his holdings transferred to cash and skip the country.''

"His family must not know that. His son showed up at Mitchell's hunting cabin this week."

"Now that was me."

"You were Peter Rucker?"

"Yeah. And I was a blind man at the airport. And an old woman in Carmelita's. Good, aren't I? Of course, you lost me when you left Carmelita's. You were on your own until I found you at the cabin."

"But how did you know we were there?"

"Mitchell told me to check it out, just in case."

"Good old Mitchell. Why didn't you arrest me then?"

"Mitchell was convinced you hadn't sold out to the enemy, but I needed proof that Rucker wasn't telling the truth and that you and Sarah weren't selling that disk to Calderone. When we got word from one of our sources that Calderone and two of his best men were flying into Texas, it looked like a sure bet that you were. The DPS called in all the Confidential agents, thinking we'd be able to track Calderone's movements and catch the exchange in the act or see what else he was up to."

"Why did you leave the cabin? You could have just followed Sarah and I if you thought we were meeting with Calderone."

"I didn't leave the cabin. Where do you think the snake in the grass came from, the one that gave you the edge?"

Cody exhaled sharply, his mind boggling. "So you were the one who provided the distraction. I owe you my life. Sarah's, too."

"Glad to be of service. And glad I happened on a stick that looked enough like a snake to make it work. But you're the one who saved the both of you. I might have gotten one of the men in the time you took out all three. That would have left two of them to kill you and Sarah.''

''I'm just glad it's over. Glad Sarah's safe. But I still wish I knew what happened to that disk we lost. The code could be floating around anywhere.''

''I wouldn't worry about that. That wasn't the real code. We switched the file out for a fake one about a week before Sarah copied it, right after Kendra discovered that the leak in the DPS was real and not just a suspicion. Only Mitchell and a few top guys in the Washington DPS office knew I was working on this, or even alive. We weren't ready to rule out anyone.''

''Except Mitchell.'' Cody finished his beer, still trying to make sense of everything. ''I guess I shouldn't be surprised that the powers in charge of the DPS thought I might be guilty of selling out to the enemy. My past speaks for itself.''

''You've been in a scrape or two. Mitchell, however, never doubted you. He just felt bad that he'd put you in a position to jump in Calderone's way.''

''Why is that?''

''Why don't you ask him?'' Daniel pushed up his sleeve and glanced at his watch. ''If you hurry you can make it before visiting hours are over. He just got word that they moved the surgery up to tomorrow morning. He asked me not to tell anyone and spoil the celebration, but I know he'd like to see you.''

Cody felt a hand on his arm. He hadn't even noticed when Sarah had moved down to sit beside him.

''Do it,'' she urged. ''Go see him.''

He nodded. ''I guess it's time to face the truth head-on.''

THE HOSPITAL corridor seemed a hundred miles long. The praise that had echoed in Cody's brain a few minutes ago had been sucked up by the grinding and gnashing inside his head. A lifetime ago he'd lain awake at night, afraid, tormented, wishing anyone besides Frank Gannon had been his dad. Now, this moment, he wished Frank had been.

Frank Gannon was a miserable excuse for a man, but he didn't pretend to be anything else. Mitchell Forbes walked tall. He was a hero. A legend. But he'd walked away from the woman he'd gotten pregnant and never even bothered to see if his son needed him. Never even admitted he had a son.

The door to Mitchell's room was ajar. He stood outside for long moments, then finally pushed the door open and stepped inside.

Chapter Sixteen

"Hello, Mitchell."

Mitchell rolled over and faced him. His face was drawn, thinner than it had been a week ago. And pale, as if the color had been bleached from his weathered skin. Cody dug deep, trying to find the bitterness he'd nurtured a minute ago. But it had turned to a frayed knot in the pit of his stomach.

"I figured Maddie would be here with you tonight."

"I just ran her out. She needs some rest." He put down the lighter he'd been fiddling with when Cody walked in. "How does it feel to single-handedly accomplish something the whole DPS has been trying to do for years?"

"It wasn't exactly single-handed. I had help from Daniel Austin and from Sarah Rand."

"I know. Daniel filled me in on the details while you and Sarah were paying a call to the doctor. I know I've been hard on you at times. Probably too hard, but I've been proud of you from the day you signed on with Texas Confidential. I'm especially proud tonight."

Cody knew he should take the compliment and let it go. He couldn't. Not this time. He had to know the truth, once and for all. "What about before I signed on? Were you proud of me when you were pulling strings to get me out of trouble or to find someone to give me a decent job when I was out of work? That was you who stepped in behind the scenes, wasn't it, *Dad?*"

Mitchell flinched. "How long have you known?"

"Almost a week. I was paying you a visit here and overheard a discussion between you and Maddie."

"I didn't mean for you to find out like that."

"You didn't mean for me to find out at all."

Mitchell felt along the side of the bed until he found the control button and raised his bed to a sitting position. "There didn't seem a reason to tell you, Cody. You didn't need a father anymore. I hoped we'd be friends. I thought we were."

"Rafe was my friend. So were Brady and Jake. You were the boss, the man I never quite learned how to please."

"I made a mistake. I made lots of them."

"So have I." Cody shuffled his feet and studied the pattern the lamplight made on the wall behind Mitchell's head. "Look, I didn't come here to dig up the past. I shouldn't have said anything, not tonight. I just wanted to wish you well in surgery tomorrow."

"Sit down, Cody. This won't take long, but I have a few things that need saying."

"They can wait."

"Maybe, but I'll have a lot clearer conscience under the knife tomorrow if I say them tonight."

Cody pulled a straight-backed chair to the edge of the bed and straddled it. "Say your piece if that's what suits you."

"I don't have any excuses for what happened between me and your mother. It just did. I was eighteen when I first got stationed in Vietnam. Before I reached nineteen, I was back home, recuperating. My buddies were getting blown to bits. I turned a truck over and won an extended leave.''

"Is that when you met Mom?"

"I knew Rose before that, but we'd never dated. That summer we did. We were inseparable, couldn't stand to be apart for more than a day. She called it love. I was never sure. I just knew that when I returned to Nam, I'd go back to the front and face the same daily tragedies I had before I'd been handed the reprieve.''

"Did you ask her to marry you?"

"No, but she asked me. Every day. I turned her down. I couldn't see her sitting home twiddling her thumbs while I played soldier. I figured she'd get tired of waiting on me and find someone else, and I'd watched too many of my friends open their Dear John letters and go off the deep end. I wasn't planning to be one of them.''

"So that was that.''

"Not quite. I went back to Nam. She wrote me a couple of times, but never mentioned she was pregnant. The next thing I knew a friend of mine wrote me that Rose had married Frank Gannon and that they were expecting a child.''

"I guess that beat a Dear John letter.''

"It was a thousand times worse. I guess that's when I realized how much I loved Rose. By then it was too late.''

"But she must have told you that you were the father of her baby before she married Frank Gannon?"

"Not even a hint. She hardly even spoke to me when we ran into each other in town. Your mother was a proud woman. I just didn't know how proud until it was too late.''

''So when did you find out that you had a son?''

''I got a letter from a lawyer when you turned eighteen. An official-looking document to inform me that Cody Gannon was actually my son and that I was free to come to you with the truth if I saw fit. Apparently your mom had set all of this up before she died.''

Cody struggled with the story. ''I can't believe Mom didn't tell me herself. She knew she had cancer. She knew she wasn't going to make it.''

''I guess she didn't want to hit you with any traumatic revelations while you were dealing with her death, especially since she didn't know how I'd react to the news.''

''So you got the letter, but you still chose not to tell me the truth, not to claim the troubled kid raised by Frank Gannon as your son.''

''I figured it was eighteen years too late to become a father. I didn't know you. You didn't know me. And I didn't know the kind of life you and your mother had lived under Frank Gannon's rule. I didn't find that out until later, until I'd looked into everything about you, trying to find some way to help you get your life together.''

Tension hovered between them. Cody had held on to the bitterness from his youth for so long that it had become embedded in his soul. Even if he believed Mitchell's story, he couldn't just let it go all at once.

''I don't expect you to forgive me, Cody. There's no reason why you should. I knew when I got that first letter telling me Rose was pregnant that there was a chance the baby was mine. I didn't pursue it, didn't know how I'd be able to deal with Rose letting another man raise my son. Besides, I was still getting over a war I didn't understand. Dealing with a hell of my own I couldn't get out of my head.''

"I'm glad you told me." Cody stood and walked over to stand by the bed. "I guess a man always does what he thinks is right at the time." Even if it was to run from the thing he wanted most in his life. A woman he loved. A family.

He extended a hand to Mitchell and the old warhorse gripped it. "We'll talk later," Cody said, "but I'll be here in the morning when they wheel you into surgery."

"I'd like that. I'd like that a whole lot. Now you go out and celebrate. You deserve it."

"I will."

SARAH WAS STILL sitting in Vaqueros with the rest of the Confidential agents when Cody returned. He walked right up to her and slipped an arm around her shoulder.

"I have a toast to make," he said.

Rafe banged a half-empty beer bottle on the table. "You go, hero. You're the man."

Cody lifted his glass. "To life, love and kids. May we all share them with someone we love."

Everyone cheered and roared in agreement. Sarah simply stared at him. "What did you say?"

"That I love you. That I want to spend my life with you. That I want to be a father to your child, though I'll have to learn how." He took both of her hands in his. "Will you marry me?"

"Yes. Yes." She threw her hands up in the air, her voice rising above the din. "Yes."

He swept her into his arms and started toward the door. "Let's get out of here."

"Whatever you say, cowboy."

He stopped walking. "Only I guess we better call your mother first and tell her the news."

She smiled and wiped a tear from her eye. "There is no mother, Cody."

"Of course there is. The nurse, the missionary, the woman with all the sage advice."

"A figment of my imagination. I invented her years ago when I was being shuffled from one foster home to another, back when I needed someone to love me. So, every time I feel frightened or alone, I resurrect her."

"Then I guess you won't be needing her anymore." He kissed her then, in front of everyone. His cute, sexy, pregnant wife-to-be.

"Are there any more surprises?" he asked when he came up for air.

"A million of them."

She smiled that taunting, seductive, pouty smile that always turned him on. And Cody knew that he would love discovering every one.

Epilogue

Three Months Later
Christmas Eve

"Hey, you moved my ornament."

"It was blocking mine."

"Was not."

"Who wants egg nog?"

"Is there any of that German chocolate cake left? I'd like a piece of that."

"Anyone else hungry? There's pecan pie and marsh-mallow fudge."

"I'll take anything except that fruitcake that came in the mail today. Save that until next year and send it back to the joker who mailed it to us."

"I like fruitcake."

"You would."

Sarah squirmed, trying to find a comfortable position on the big couch at the Smoking Barrel while she took in the sights and sounds of her first family Christmas. The Texas Confidential family.

Laughter, singing, chatter, teasing, eating.

Chaos.

She absolutely loved it, even with the contractions

that had started just before she'd come down the stairs to the parlor.

A few months ago, she would have never believed everything could turn out so perfect. Cody, a Texas Confidential agent again. And he and Mitchell had made their peace, at least most of the time. They were both too hardheaded not to have a few disagreements, especially now that Mitchell had recovered so well from his surgery.

And with Daniel Austin's testimony and Marcus Slade's confessions, all charges had been dropped against her. Calderone was still awaiting trial, but the evidence was stacked solidly against him. Marcus had even admitted that he'd organized the cattle rustling at the Smoking Barrel, just to keep the Confidential agents busy and out of the way while he ran Calderone's illegal drug operations.

A perfect Christmas Eve. And her gorgeous husband sat next to her, looking at this year's Christmas card from Lauralee Miller. "It's a beautiful card," she said. "She's very artistic."

"The first female whose life I saved sent me a touching handmade card for Christmas. Wonder what the second female whose life I saved has in mind?"

She took his hand and placed it on her stomach. "This. And two o'clock feedings and dirty diapers."

Daniel Austin walked over and took a seat on the other side of her. "It's nice to see you two so happy."

"It's nice to be this happy," she agreed. "It's like stashing all your dreams in a box. Then one day you lift the lid, and they all come true."

Cody squeezed her hand. "I couldn't have said it better myself. Shorter, maybe, but not better." He turned to Daniel. "What about you? Are you planning on staying in Texas?"

"I don't know. Right now Montana looks good to me."

"Then there is something to the rumor that the DPS wants to start a Confidential branch up there."

Daniel smiled but didn't get a chance to answer. The clamor around them quieted as Mitchell stood and tapped a spoon handle against his glass. "Okay, everyone, I have something to say. Actually I have something to ask. Maddie, will you quit fooling around in that kitchen and come in here for a minute?"

She stepped inside the door, her green eyes flashing. "If you've bought me another silly Christmas present like that shirt with a bikini painted on it, I'm not opening it."

"Nope, this is something you might even wear."

She groaned. "I'm afraid to look."

He pulled a ring box from his pocket and lifted the lid. The room grew totally silent. "I'm tired of all your pestering. So, I'm finally asking."

She stared at him without batting an eye.

"Will you marry me?" he asked, his voice suddenly gruff.

She cocked her head to one side and planted her hands on her hips. "Does that proposal come with an 'I love you'?"

"Would I be proposing marriage if I didn't?"

She crossed the room and stepped into his arms. "That's not the most romantic proposal in the world, but I'll take it. The answer is yes."

Everyone cheered and squealed in delight. All except Sarah. She just squealed. "It's time, Cody."

He glanced at his watch. "It's still early."

"No. I mean, it's time for your present."

"The baby?"

She nodded. It was time. For her and for Cody and for Joy—for all their lives.

Don't miss Penny's story,

THE SECRETARY GETS HER MAN,

by Mindy Neff

**Coming next month from
Harlequin American Romance!**

Turn the page for a sneak peek!

**And look for
MONTANA CONFIDENTIAL,**

coming in August 2001.

Chapter One

Penny Archer stepped a little harder on the throttle of her sleek black Cadillac as the headlights caught the reflective road sign announcing Darby, Texas, five miles ahead.

Along the gravel shoulder of the road a deer paused, eyes shining bright in the flash of headlights. Penny eased up on the gas. She'd been traveling for close to six hours and it wouldn't do to play a game of chicken with the wildlife. From experience, she knew the Caddie would end up on the losing end of the deal if it came down to a collision.

And it would only set her back timewise. In and out, she promised herself. She'd get her grandmother's affairs in order, sell the house, touch base with a couple of her high school friends, then get the heck out of Dodge—or Darby, rather.

She wondered if she'd subconsciously chosen the cover of darkness to return to her hometown that she'd visited only twice in the past twelve years.

Memories rolled over her—some painful, some embarrassing and some that were gentle, warm and irreplaceable.

She felt bad that she hadn't been here for her grandmother's funeral. Agnes Archer had been a pistol of a woman, tough to get along with, bitter, but nobody deserved to die and be buried alone. If it hadn't been for the latest case the Texas Confidential unit had been working on, Penny would have come. But she'd been tied up and the funeral had taken place without her.

Uncharacteristically, Penny flipped down the visor and checked her appearance in the lighted mirror as she turned onto Main Street. The image staring back at her gave her an instant's jolt. An hour back, when she'd stopped for gas, she'd impulsively exchanged her stylish, wire-rimmed glasses for a pair of contact lenses. Vanity wasn't normally part of her makeup, but some devil had urged Penny to take off the glasses, to play up her assets, to show off the good bone structure she'd enhanced with a little cosmetics.

Annoyed with herself, she flipped the visor back in place. It was dark as sin out, for heaven's sake. The sidewalks in town had no doubt been rolled up by five, and it was after eleven now. Not another soul was on the road. Who did she expect to see? Or impress?

An image of a boy with dark hair, broad shoulders and gentle brown eyes flashed like a strobe in her brain and she immediately cut it off. Her life was on a different course now and there wasn't room for foolish fantasies.

For the past twelve years Penny had been working as Mitchell Forbes's executive assistant in the highly secretive Texas Confidential organization. She knew the cases and the agents better than anyone. And although her position with the Confidentials was important and fulfilling, lately Penny had yearned for more. She hadn't quite been able to put her finger on what that "more" was until she'd single-handedly apprehended a band of cattle rustlers who'd been plaguing the Smoking Barrel ranch for months. The adrenaline rush, the sense of accomplishment and the recognition and praise she'd gotten from her friends and colleagues had given her the courage to tell Mitchell she wanted a more active role in the agency.

She wanted to be an agent.

Mitchell had agreed, and by this time next month, she would begin her training. But first she had to take care of her grandmother's estate.

And perhaps, to a certain degree, Penny needed to face up to her past before she could actually move on. Where that thought came from, she had no idea. And it made her more than a little uncomfortable.

Through the Cadillac's heavily tinted windows, she gazed out at the dark storefronts where shadowy mannequins posing in the boutiques seemed to follow the progress of her car as she passed. The crazy thought had Penny laughing out loud. She'd obviously been hanging around secret agents too long—needed a vacation more than she'd realized. She was starting to see menace in plastic dummies in store windows.

A banner stretching across the street from opposite light poles announced the coming of the Fourth of July parade. Three weeks away. Where had the year gone already?

Leaving the quiet streets of town, she wound her way through a tree-lined residential area and turned into the driveway of her grandmother's wood-and-brick house. Two strips of concrete represented the driveway. Untended grass growing along the centre of the drive brushed the Cadillac's undercarriage. Behind the house, the detached garage loomed like a big old barn—with a padlock threaded through the hinge. Evidently Grandma hadn't gotten around to installing the automatic garage-door opener Penny had sent.

When she shut off the engine, silence pressed in on her. She was used to living on an isolated ranch, listening to the sounds of animals and insects and nature. She was used to being alone—or at least single. Tonight the quiet unnerved her.

She reached for her purse and got out of the car, digging through the bag as she went up the back porch steps. When her fingers didn't touch the set of keys she was certain she'd put there, she used a penlight to search the interior of the leather pocketbook, then ended up dumping the contents on the porch.

Great. She'd forgotten the darn keys the attorney had mailed to her. That wasn't like her. She was efficient to a fault—she had to be to run a highly secretive agency like the Texas Confidentials. Well, not exactly run it, but close to it. She was their right-hand woman—albeit behind the scenes. But all that was about to change.

Running her hands above the door and along the sides of the shutters, she searched for a spare key, knowing she wasn't likely to find one. Agnes Archer had been a private, paranoid woman. In a town where most people never locked their doors, Agnes had installed double dead bolts. She wouldn't have set out a spare key for some criminal to find.

Penny often wondered why her grandmother had been so fixated on criminals to begin with.

Unable to jimmy the windows that had been virtually painted shut over the years, Penny knew the only way she was going to get in and get any rest was to break a window. Going back to the car, she retrieved her tire iron and a blanket she kept in the trunk for emergencies.

Although she was prepared for the sound, she cringed as shattering glass rained inside against the pine wood floor. Wrapping her hand and arm in the blanket, she cleared the jagged edges away, then climbed through the opening onto the service porch.

Agnes had been gone for over two weeks now, but the clean, familiar scent of starch still lingered. The narrow beam of her flashlight passed over the ironing board sitting in the corner, the iron resting facedown amid a rusty brown water stain.

Entering the kitchen, Penny slapped at the light switch, distressed when the power didn't come on. She was tired, her nerves were rawer than she'd anticipated and she wasn't in the mood to stumble around in a dark house that evoked more emotions than she cared to feel.

Hoping it was just a burned-out bulb, she went into the living room and tried the lamp, knocking her shin against the end tale and barely suppressing a curse.

When that light didn't come on either, she tried to recall where the circuit breaker panel was.

"Hold it right there."

Fear, primal and burning, stole her breath and shot through her blood with a dizzying jolt. For a fleeting, hysterical instant her thought was that this was the wrong reaction for a government agent to have. Never mind that she wasn't a full-fledged agent yet. She should be deadly calm, ready to act and react.

Belatedly, though no more than a second could have passed, Penny whirled around, simultaneously shutting off the pitifully weak beam of the flashlight so as not to make herself a target. Her eyes not yet adjusted to the inky blackness, she crouched and reached for the gun in her purse. But before she could even register that her pocketbook wasn't hanging at her side, a shoulder slammed into her midsection and she went down hard, her hip jarring against the unyielding wood floor.

Finesse gave way to sheer terror and self-preservation as she squirmed and kicked and jabbed. "You son of a—"

"Wait! Hold it…"

"Not a chance, buddy." She arched beneath her assailant. Unable to get good enough leverage to throw a decent punch, she started to bring her knee up.

"Hold on, wildcat…damn it…Penny, it's me."

He didn't have to identify who "me" was.

Memories flashed.

That voice. A voice she hadn't heard in sixteen years.

The voice of the only man she'd ever truly loved— or thought she'd loved—a man who'd made a fool of her and broken her heart, a man who'd proved what her grandmother had spent nearly a lifetime drumming into Penny's head. That men were no good and not to be trusted with her heart.

Joe Colter.

HARLEQUIN®
INTRIGUE
opens the case files on:

Unwrap the mystery!

January 2001
#597 THE BODYGUARD'S BABY
Debra Webb

February 2001
#601 SAVING HIS SON
Rita Herron

March 2001
#605 THE HUNT FOR HAWKE'S DAUGHTER
Jean Barrett

April 2001
#609 UNDERCOVER BABY
Adrianne Lee

May 2001
#613 CONCEPTION COVER-UP
Karen Lawton Barrett

Follow the clues to your favorite retail outlet.

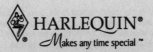

Visit us at www.eHarlequin.com

HITSB

If you enjoyed what you just read,
then we've got an offer you can't resist!

Take 2 bestselling love stories FREE!

Plus get a FREE surprise gift!

Clip this page and mail it to Harlequin Reader Service®

IN U.S.A.	IN CANADA
3010 Walden Ave.	P.O. Box 609
P.O. Box 1867	Fort Erie, Ontario
Buffalo, N.Y. 14240-1867	L2A 5X3

YES! Please send me 2 free Harlequin Intrigue® novels and my free surprise gift. Then send me 4 brand-new novels every month, which I will receive before they're available in stores. In the U.S.A., bill me at the bargain price of $3.57 plus 25¢ delivery per book and applicable sales tax, if any*. In Canada, bill me at the bargain price of $3.96 plus 25¢ delivery per book and applicable taxes**. That's the complete price and a savings of at least 10% off the cover prices— what a great deal! I understand that accepting the 2 free books and gift places me under no obligation ever to buy any books. I can always return a shipment and cancel at any time. Even if I never buy another book from Harlequin, the 2 free books and gift are mine to keep forever. So why not take us up on our invitation. You'll be glad you did!

181 HEN C22Y

381 HEN C22Z

Name	(PLEASE PRINT)	
Address	Apt.#	
City	State/Prov.	Zip/Postal Code

* Terms and prices subject to change without notice. Sales tax applicable in N.Y.
** Canadian residents will be charged applicable provincial taxes and GST.
   All orders subject to approval. Offer limited to one per household.
   ® are registered trademarks of Harlequin Enterprises Limited.

INT00

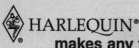

HARLEQUIN®
AMERICAN ◆ ROMANCE®

and **Muriel Jensen**

present

WHO'S THE DADDY?

*A*t a festive costume ball, three identical
sisters meet three masked bachelors.

*E*ach couple has a taste of true love behind
the anonymity of their costumes—but
only one will become parents
in nine months!

Find out who it will be!

November 2000
FATHER FEVER #858

January 2001
FATHER FORMULA #855

March 2001
FATHER FOUND #866

HARLEQUIN®
*M*akes any time special ™

TEXAS CONFIDENTIAL

Penny Archer has always been the dependable and hardworking executive assistant for Texas Confidential, a secret agency of Texas lawmen. But her daring heart yearned to be the heroine of her own adventure—and to find a love that would last a lifetime.

And this time...

THE SECRETARY GETS HER MAN
by Mindy Neff

Coming in January 2001 from

 HARLEQUIN®

AMERICAN *Romance*

If you missed the TEXAS CONFIDENTIAL series from Harlequin Intrigue, you can place an order with our Customer Service Department.

Visit us at www.eHarlequin.com

HARTC